Chapter One: Curios

Meg was bored. Oh, sure, reconstruction had begun, thanks to an anonymous donor, so it wasn't like there wasn't anything to look at. But when one has been around set constructions and the like all their life, it gets tiresome. It would be easier if Christine was there. At least then there would have been someone to talk to and share her boredom. But after she and Raul escaped the Phantom's lair somehow, she kept to herself and her wedding plans. Had it really been three weeks? Three weeks since she had watched the Phantom kidnap Christine right before her eyes(and the eyes of every other person in the opera house)? Three weeks since she had led a mob into the dark caverns and come across the Phantom's infamous white mask?

The search had been officially called off one week later, although with the fire going, it hadn't really lasted very long. And even after the flames were put out, only a trickle of people had gone back down to search for the Opera Ghost. Now, everyone was satisfied just from the lack of pranks, threats, and notes. Everyone except for Meg, that is.

Sure, he may have murdered and kidnapped and blackmailed and manipulated, but he had been a constant in her life at the opera house. Someone she could always count on, even though he was random and unpredictable. There was a huge mystery about him that Meg had always found fascinating. Even after that fateful night when Christine had yanked off his mask, Meg still knew nothing about him. Sometimes, she thought she didn't want to know more. Other times, the questions were so forefront in her mind, but she couldn't ask anyone about him. Certainly not Christine, for the mere mention of him sent her into a silent trance. Her mother was out—once when she was around five or six, she had asked Madame Giry who the Opera Ghost was, and her mother had shushed her sternly.

Growing tired of sitting there alone with her thoughts, Meg left the dorm room and went looking for her mother; perhaps she could help her come up with a new routine to work on. But as she entered Madame Giry's bedchamber, she found it empty. She shrugged and sat down on her mother's bed. *She has to come back here sometime...* she thought with a sigh. It was then she saw a pile of old "O.G." notes on the bedside table. *These should prove entertaining...* Grinning, she picked up the top note, and as she read it, she realized it was one she had never seen before.

" *To my one and only friend,*

As I am eternally in your debt for all you have done for me all these years, I feel that I should give you warning. I think you know, as do I, that things are getting out of hand. I wish I knew how to control it, but I am at a loss. All I can think about is how much I love Christine. I feel that the more I act on my feelings for her, the more I am failing you. I am truly sorry for that, but I don't see any other option. The least I can do is this. If things go the way I suspect they will, I want you to use my salary money that you have deposited for me to fix anything that needs it. I'm sorry I can't give you anymore detail than that. You have been a loyal friend that I do not deserve, Antoinette. Know that I am eternally grateful for that. I'm sorry.

Your friend,

E. "

So, was this the anonymous donor that was paying for the repairs? And could this 'E' be the Phantom?

"Meg, what are you doing here?" Mme. Giry interrupted her thoughts, and Meg immediately jumped to her feet.

"I was, uh, looking for you..." she grinned sheepishly.

"What were you doing reading my private messages, hmm?"

"I...uh...I'm going to go...stretch..." Meg tossed the letter onto the bed and slid past her mother's glare.

"Just stay out of the way of the workers!" Mme. Giry warned, but Meg was already halfway down the corridor. Obviously, if she was going to get to the bottom of this mystery once and for all, she knew exactly what she needed to do. After all, Meg had found the Phantom's mask. He couldn't have gone too far without it, could he? Her heart beat faster as she returned to her dorm room to retrieve the mask from under her pillow. As she picked it up, her hand tingled for a moment as she remembered the first time she had seen him. It had been right after Joseph Buquet's murder. She had looked up from where he had fallen, and there was the Phantom, glaring down at the stage. Even now, it seemed as though she was touching his face. *Pull yourself together, Meg. It's just a mask, it won't bite you.* Taking a deep breath, she crept out of the room and toward Christine's dressing room. If she was going to do this, she needed to do it now.

Erik lay on the cold stone floor, shivering. How long had be been here? A month? Two days? What did it matter anymore? For the millionth time, he contemplated just ending it all, but now he was too weak to move from his spot. It seemed to him that he had been there forever, never-ending tears flowing down his face for the love he had lost. Even now, as he thought of her, new tears began to flow, even though his mouth and throat was dry, even though hunger pained his sides. Surely he would die here. A long painful death was surely what he felt he deserved. Even if he didn't, the world surely did. Sometimes he wished he hadn't gone into hiding, just so they could have found him and ended it right then and there. *Too late now*, he thought. All he could do now was wait for death to find him. *At least death will keep me company*, he thought bitterly.

Chapter Two: A Discovery

As Meg neared the bottom of the staircase, she wondered if she was doing the right thing. After all, she had narrowly missed falling through a trap door into who-knows-what until who-knows-when. And there was no telling as to how many more traps she might encounter. As she turned around, however, she realized that she really didn't feel like climbing all those stairs again. Not to mention she had forgotten which step was the trap one. She turned around and took the last couple steps down into the cavern. Moving her torch around, she saw that there was a huge underground lake right in front of her. A small boat sat on a bank about ten feet to her right, but she would have to get wet in order to get to it. *Mama is going to kill me.* Having no knowledge of the depth of the water, nor the willingness to turn back, she gingerly stepped into the water. *Cold, cold, oh cold!* She all but jumped right into the boat and pushed off.

Once she got further into the lake, her surroundings became vaguely familiar. Finally she rounded a corner and came face-to-face with the Phantom's living quarters. The candles had been left burning all this time; only a fraction were still lit, and even then, she knew they would go out any day now. She was thankful for thinking to bring the torch along as she stepped out of the boat and onto dry land. Once again, she approached the table where the little monkey toy sat, and as she examined it, she realized it was a music box. Grinning, she wound it up.

Christine towered over his shivering form, laughing with the crowd around them. She bent down only to yank his mask off, and then raised the whip. *No, Christine! No!* But his voice was silent compared to the laughs and jeers, and he braced himself for the blows that were to come. He didn't know what hurt worse—the sound of her laughs or the pain from each snap of the whip. Either way, he could not take it much longer. Fresh tears began to flow, and he found his voice once again. "NOOO! CHRISTINE, WHY?" Erik screamed into the darkness.

What on earth was that? Meg jumped at the sound of almost inhuman wails. She followed the sound to a dark red velvet curtain, and as she pulled it aside, she gasped. *So this is where you've been hiding,* she smiled triumphantly. But as his sobs grew louder, her smile faded and she could feel her heart breaking at the sound. *The poor man. The poor lonely man...* Cautiously, she brought her torch through the doorway and into the passageway. After what seemed like fifteen minutes, the silhouette of a sleeping man came into view, and she knelt down beside him. No, he wasn't sleeping. He was sobbing and shaking. Slowly, she brought her hand to his shoulder. Almost instantly, his hand grabbed onto her wrist, and he pulled her over himself, throwing her off-balance and onto the stone floor. The torch flew out of her hand deeper into the tunnel, but she could not think about that. Tears welled up in her eyes as she held her wrist to her chest. She mentally kicked herself. *Of course he would defend himself, stupid girl! He's been in here for weeks, half starved!* Slowly, she crawled back over to him. "Sir? Phantom? Can you hear me?" her voice was little more than a whisper, but she refused to speak any louder for fear of startling him again. Her wrist throbbed in pain, and she bit her lip and put up a brave front.

"Christine...I'm so sorry, Christine! I'm so sorry..." he mumbled.

"Phantom, it's Meg...Meg Giry. Christine isn't here..." Instinctively she pulled away; one injured wrist was quite enough for one day. He did not respond, however. He was spending far too much time shaking and shivering. Food. He needed food and warmth. Meg quickly stood and, retrieving the torch, she made her way back out of the tunnel. She hurriedly found some thick blankets on his massive bed and rushed to get them to him. As soon as she had covered his pitiful form, the amount of shivers quickly decreased. He was still sobbing though, and Meg felt her own tears begin to flow freely now. She went back to the Phantom's living quarters and found a small piece of cloth to wrap her wrist up in. It was a start, at least, and she sat down on the bed. Night had surely fallen by now, and she was reluctant to find her way back through the passageways at this late hour.

As she lay down, thoughts of the Phantom passed through her mind. Who was this man? This man who killed without hesitation, and yet was generous enough to pay for the damage he had yet to cause. This man who obviously loved Christine more than life itself, and yet was kind enough to let her be with Raul, the one she loved. The more she thought of him, the more mysterious he became.

Chapter Three: Nightmares and Dreams

When Meg woke up, she felt refreshed and ready to face the plan she had worked out in her sleep. *If only my wrist would stop throbbing...*she winced as she was reminded of her injury. She approached the lake and dipped her wrist into the coolness of it. She could not linger very long; the

Phantom needed food three weeks ago. She dried her wrist off and wrapped it in fresh cloth, then grasped the torch. After some searching, she found fresh candles in a drawer and soon had the cave well-lit. Smiling triumphantly, she then decided to explore some of the smaller caverns. Surely he would have food stored somewhere.

After trying three caverns, she finally came across one that had a small fireplace against a wall. Along the opposite wall were shelves lined with loaves of bread, a few vegetables, and some fish. She found a cooking pot and a few hand-carved dishes on another shelf, and quickly began preparing a watery stew. *Not much*, she thought, *but one who is hungry cannot afford to be picky.*

So, you've come to show me off again, Erik sneered. *Christine did not respond as she dragged him back into the enclosure. A new day, a new crowd, same pain and torture. Christine ripped his mask off his head again, then ripped it into a thousand pieces. Sneering, she raised the whip again. NOO! NOT AGAIN! Something inside Erik snapped, but he was bound in chains so heavy he could not move.* "CHRISTINE!"

Meg paused mid-step as soon as she heard his voice. *Poor, tortured man!* Her pace quickened now, though she was careful as to not spill the meager meal. It was the first thing she had ever cooked, and she wondered how she had gone through with it. There was no time for self-doubt, however, for she had reached his side once again. Slowly, so as not to touch him, she knelt down beside his head and lifted the spoon to his mouth. *Please eat it!* She pleaded. The first mouthful dribbled out the corners of his lips, but that was to be expected. Patiently, she tried again.

She was drowning him. That was the only explanation. *Fine. Go ahead. Drown me. Put me out of* *my misery.* He smirked bravely. His mouth went under again, however, and he felt panic take over. He coughed and sputtered, but something caught in his mouth. *A...carrot?* Erik chewed slowly, savoring every morsel. *Don't mock me, woman! Either drown me or feed me but for goodness sake no more torture!* Another mouthful of the liquid, and this time he tasted potatoes and fish.

Soon, the bowl was empty, and Meg set it down with a smile. She watched as his mouth seemed to still be searching for another taste. "Phantom? It's me, Meg. Can you hear me?" Silence. The only response she got was the wrinkling of his eyebrows in confusion. "I'm going to get some more stew, Phantom. Rest now." How she longed to place a reassuring hand on his pale face! But the thought escaped her mind as quickly as it had appeared as her wrist began screaming with pain again.

Three bowls of stew later, the Phantom finally seemed to be finished with his breakfast, and Meg ate the fourth bowl herself. Now that he was resting peacefully, she moved the torch slightly closer in order to study him better. His hands were covered in speckles of dried blood, and she wondered if that had been caused by him breaking all his mirrors. Sweat and tears soaked his face, and he began shaking again. Without touching him, she could tell immediately that he had a fever, and she leaped over him to get another small cloth soaked with cold water.

Ah, my mask. You fixed it, Erik half-smiled, then let it fade. *You couldn't have dried it first? Wait, no! My hands aren't in need of a mask! What are you doing woman? Make up your mind! Stop torturing me!*

He let out a soft moan as she dabbed at his cut hands, but she could not stop. Finally, the wounds were clean, and she placed the cloth into the bowl of water again. She gingerly put her hand on his forehead, and was surprised when he didn't react. Slowly, she allowed her hand to caress his face. Slowly, he moved his hand up to touch hers, and she nearly choked up her heart. *Way to go, Meg. You just had to press your luck, didn't you?* But he did not harm her this time. Instead, he took her hand gently into his. "Stay with me." he whispered. She stared down at him for a moment. His eyes were still closed. Did he know who she was? *Think, Meg, think!* But all that came to her mind was how much her mother was going to kill her.

"Phantom? I'm Meg...do you hear me?" She tugged at her hand, but he gently squeezed it.

"Don't go..." He was breathing evenly now, and she knew he had fallen asleep, clutching her hand tightly to his chest. *Oh Mama please forgive me...* Meg lowered herself to the cold floor, keeping a wide space between them.

Chapter Four: Angel of Death, Angel of Life

So, you've come at last to keep me company, Death. I bid you welcome. Please stay a while. I don't have visitors often. Even when I do, they always end up leaving. You won't leave me, will you? Will you not answer me? But of course. Death is always silent. But at least I won't be alone. You've grown cold. But that's to be expected, is it not?

Meg shivered and opened her eyes. Had she gone to sleep? Yes, she must have, for the torch fire was little more than the tiniest glow. She must refresh the flame. Not to mention the Phantom must be hungry again. She sat up and immediately felt the stiffness in her back on top of the throbbing pain in her wrist. It was then she remembered that he was clutching her other hand. *Oh, why won't you wake up?* She made another attempt to free herself, but he moaned and held her tighter. "Take me with you!" Meg would have argued and tried once again to introduce herself to him, but she was hungry and tired of all this nonsense.

"Alright, but you must get up and walk yourself. I can't carry you."

"So you do speak." The Phantom moved into a sitting position.

"Of course I do. I've been speaking to you all this time." Meg watched as he stood, keeping her hand locked in his grip. Meg knelt to pick up the torch, then led him out of the tunnel and to the bed. "You must lie down here." He did as he was told. "Can you not open your eyes, Phantom?"

Phantom? *Oh, Death, will you not use my real name?* But then, he had hidden himself behind the Phantom mask so much that he shouldn't be very surprised. *What did you say? Open my eyes? Why should I? Why should I take a last look at the world that showed me no mercy or compassion? Or perhaps we have already left it. Is that it?* Slowly, he lifted his eyelids. A blurry figure came into view, but before he could get a better look, pain rushed to his eyes, and he quickly shut them.

"Oh, dear, they are quite swollen, aren't they?" While he brought his hands up to his eyes, Meg took the opportunity to slip away and proceeded to dip a clean cloth into the lake. Upon her return, she laid the cloth over his eyes, gently dabbing at the redness and swelling. When she was done, she set the cloth on his forehead. "Now, let's try that again, shall we? Open them again." Slowly, he opened them again.

*Funny. **This place looks** so familiar, Death. Or was I right all along about living in it all these years? But wait. You're not Death! You're...* "Meg? Meg Giry?" He felt his throat burn at the effort to speak.

"Yes...welcome back."

"What makes you think I want to be back?" Dazed and confused or not, the bitterness was forefront in his voice.

"I'm sorry, but I couldn't just sit there watching you die, Phantom. Speaking of which, I'll fetch some more stew right away." Before he could respond, she was gone, and Erik wondered again if this was all just a dream. It had to be. But no, the coolness on his forehead was real, and he reached up to remove the cloth. Oh, but it felt so good, and so he put it back.

"You'll have to sit up again so I can feed you. I can't have you choking your lunch up." Meg sat down beside his head. As he ate, she couldn't help noticing him watching her with confusion in his deep green eyes. As soon as the bowl was empty, he placed his hand on her arm before she could get back up. *Oh here we go again...* "Yes?" She fought the urge to roll her eyes.

"Did Antoi—your mother send you here?"

"No. Actually she has no idea I'm down here."

"I didn't think so. Why would she send you to nurse me back to health after all I did?" Erik lowered the rest of himself to the mattress. "You should return to her. I'm not worth your time or her worry. Forget about me." Before Meg could argue, he had fallen back to sleep. She let out a sigh and returned to the tunnel to retrieve the blanket. After pulling it up around him, she went to get her own supper.

***Trapped under a** net of chains again. So, Christine, you disguised yourself as Death just to drag me back, did you? I didn't think you cared. After all, what would your precious Vicomte think?Not that it matters, of course. I always knew you would come over* *to my side, my dear Christine. Come to me, my Angel of Music...*

As soon as Meg heard him moaning and thrashing about, she ran to his side. "Christine! Christine, why won't you come to me?" He wailed.

"Phantom! Phantom! Wake up! You're having a nightmare!" Meg gently shook him, and his hands felt around for her's.

"Christine..." Her friend's name came out as a sigh of relief.

"No, I'm Meg, remember?" He opened his eyes then, and they were immediately filled with disappointment.

"Leave me." He growled and turned onto his side away from her. Meg stood there for a few moments, then decided to take this time to soak her wrist again. As she let the cold water numb the pain, she contemplated where she was going to sleep. The boat was on enough land that she could sleep there with no worry of floating off. She had given him the only extra blanket, however, but she wasn't about to wrestle him for it. After all, it had been her decision to come down here. No need for him to suffer anymore than he had to just so she could be comfortable. Redressing her wrist, she got into the boat, letting the rocking motion lull her to sleep.

The next several days proved just as frustrating. She lost count as to how many times she was mistaken for Christine, but by the morning, she had learned how to wake him and then move away quickly enough to dodge his searching hands. If he didn't feel her, he opened his eyes, saw her, cursed, and then went back to sleep. She also learned to only wake him if it sounded as though he really was being tortured by his nightmares. Sometimes he stayed awake long enough to be fed, but other times he allowed himself to skip meals. Meg soon grew tired of the same stew, and she began serving him a plate of food and a bowl of water. Food was running out, however, and so the meals became smaller and smaller. Meg knew she would have to go back up into the opera house sooner or later, but she also knew that her mother would keep a closer eye on her once she did. Then where would the Phantom be? *I'm sorry, Mama, but I did not bring him out of his dying state only for him to go right back into it,* she imagined herself saying. Imagining was not the same as actually acting on it, she knew, but it was the truth. Perhaps she could lead him up and into her mother's quarters where they both could keep an eye on him, but she quickly dismissed the notion. He would be arrested for sure. But wait. He had delivered countless notes before, hadn't he? Surely she could do the same thing, if she could keep him sane enough to give her directions through the passageways. But as she watched him toss and turn in his sleep, she filed that idea away in the back of her mind as well. He was still too far gone to be of any help in that matter. No, whatever plan she came up with, she would have to act on her own.

Erik's stomach growled, and he woke up. He remained in a state of shock for a few moments—for once, hunger, not Meg, had awoken him from a surprisingly dreamless sleep. *Of course she left. You told her to, didn't you?* But as he slowly raised himself into a sitting position, his eyes soon found her sleeping form in the bottom of the boat. *Well that's a poor excuse of a bed.* The longer he stared, however, the clearer it became that she was not going to wake up anytime soon. *Well that's fine with me. I spent all my life getting things for myself. I don't need a tiny little nuisance of a ballet dancer to wait on him hand and foot.* He swung his legs over the side of the bed and stood up. He nearly collapsed again, dizzy from his illness as well as hunger. But he would not, *WOULD NOT*, allow himself to admit defeat. At least, not while Meg was down here. As soon as she tired of playing nursemaid, he would gladly see her off, and then let nature take its course.

As he shuffled into his kitchen cavern, he saw the reason for his hunger. Not a single bread crumb remained on the shelves or in the pots and pans she had used to cook in. His near starvation had caused him to require more than double the portions she had taken for herself. *And if you hadn't shown up, little Meg, I would still have at least a little food left!* As soon as the bitter thought rose, however, he realized that had she not come, he would be dead. *And what's so wrong with that? Why on earth do I need to linger here any longer? What do I have to live for, hmm? Christine is gone! Gone!* "GONE!" Tiny footsteps could be heard shuffling into the cavern behind him.

"Yes, the food is gone. I'm sorry you had to make that discovery yourself. Really, Monsieur Phantom, you must get back to bed." Erik clenched his fists and gritted his teeth. *How wrong you are, Meg, in your assumptions!* He could have laughed aloud and then broken down into sobs right then and there, but pride took over.

"No, Little Giry, the food is not gone. Had you only gone through this doorway, you would have found an underground stream full of fish." He waved his hand towards a narrow, dark doorway, smirking.

"Oh." Meg looked thoroughly defeated, causing him to smirk even wider. He passed through the doorway and grabbed a couple of tiny lassos from a peg on the wall, and within minutes, he had snared a couple of large-sized fish. Entering the kitchen once again, he all but flung the catch at Meg.

"Two things, Little Giry. One, my name is Erik. Two, I'll be expecting my breakfast in half an hour. You chose this fate, now embrace it!" With that, he stormed back into the main cave, refusing to look back at her defeated form.

This was definitely out of her comfort zone, Meg realized as she stuck the knife into the fish. She nearly lost it as the odor reached her nose. She was most definitely tired of nothing but fish! But she could not complain. She would not give him the slightest opportunity to gloat at her defeat. Tears stung her eyes. Yes, she had chose this, hadn't she? And she really could not expect him to show any gratitude after living alone all his life. She prepared the meal emotionlessly, and with five minutes to spare, she plopped the steaming plate into his lap. Not missing a beat, she carried her own meal down to the boat and ate with her back to him. "What, you aren't going to feed me this time?" She could hear the sneer in his voice.

"If you're healthy enough to kill a couple of fish, you're healthy enough to feed yourself!" *No, Meg. Don't let him get to you!* She was relieved when he did not respond, as she didn't trust her emotions at the moment.

Chapter Five: To Be Needed

Antoinette Giry scowled at the mirror. Oh, she knew where her daughter was, all right. It was the only other place she could think of as she hadn't looked there yet. She could not find fault in Meg for her curiosity. After all, she herself had been the cause for it, what with her frequent disappearing acts and secrets. Perhaps that one night when Meg had discovered this passageway, she had thought it had been one that her mother used. But no, Antoinette had gotten there quickly enough to stop her daughter from finding out the truth. She had always, *always*, protected Meg from her old friend. She had even managed to make him give his word to stay away from Meg. She had *thought* that her constant warnings and looks of disapproval would keep Meg from...this very thing.

She began pacing the floor, a heated debate going on in her mind. She knew she had to protect Meg, and the more days that passed, the more worried she became. But the mere thought of descending into his private, dark chambers scared her to death. For one thing, the cellars of the opera house were so dark and great in number, it was a wonder how Erik had managed to find his way at all. For another thing, she knew the various traps he had set as a precaution against trespassers, but she did not know where exactly each one was. Which caused her to worry even more about her daughter's welfare. But if Antoinette went down there blindly, what good would come from two victims trapped forever in the caverns? No, she had far too many things to busy her day with, between keeping the dancers occupied and practicing while the construction went on and Christine's wedding plans. Tears welled up in her eyes as she realized she was no less trapped upstairs than she would certainly be if she entered the caverns. But if she stayed here, she would not be as missed. Sighing in defeat, she realized that all she could do was pray.

This was getting tricky. He was not used to having someone to order around in his home and under his watchful eyes. But he had to keep the little sneaky dancer occupied. However, he was quickly running out of chores for her to do, not to mention she was very clever. As soon as she realized he was strong enough to do something, she flat out refused to have any part of it. Even if he feigned weakness, she would immediately point out another task of greater difficulty he had accomplished not ten minutes before. Sleep would be his only escape from her nagging, but he knew what awaited him should he attempt it. So he sat on his bed, a constant scowl on his face, teeth gritted, fists clenched.

He reminded himself that he could always turn to his music. It had always been a release from his anger. But no. His music belonged to Christine. It had been hers ever since she'd arrived at the opera house, and it would always be hers. He felt his heart ache at the thought of her, and tears came once again to his eyes. Why had he ever let her go? Why had he ever allowed himself to see the truth in her love for Raul? As soon as the Vicomte's name came to his mind, he let out a low growl. Meg looked up at him then, and he let daggers fly from his eyes at her. "Are the dishes washed, Little Giry?"

"They've been washed for an hour."

"When's supper?"

"You just ate."

There she goes *again!* He wanted to punch something. He wanted to strangle something. Anything. He slammed his fist into the massive headboard, then roared in pain.

"You really must do something about that temper of yours." That did it. Promises or not, he would *not* allow her to speak to him in that tone. He rose to his feet and walked over to where she was kneeling on the floor. He made sure he was so close that he towered over her.

"My dear, I do not think you have even seen the *half* of my temper!" He raised his hand to strike her face, and she didn't even wince. She met his gaze evenly, daring him to hit her. Those eyes...those eyes so similar to those of Antoinette's. He clenched up his fist and stormed back to the bed, injured but not defeated. "Get a bucket and a cloth and scrub the floors. All of them. That will teach you to be so insolent!" He was pleased to see her quick to obey his orders. She would learn, sooner or later. He would break her. If he couldn't bring himself to act in violence against her, he would tame her using other means.

A new figure stepped in front of the cowering masked boy. He and Christine both held sticks in their hands. Both wore sneers on their faces. Christine struck first, but her fiance wasn't too far behind. With each blow, a new spark of anger was born until a raging fire took over. Erik rushed forward, snapping the rope that had kept him tethered to the iron bars. Screaming, he lunged at Raul and grabbed him by the throat, knocking him to the floor. No more. "No more!"

Meg sputtered, gasping for breath while grabbing a hold of Erik's wrists. "Erik! Wake...up!" He was almost all the way on top of her, using his full weight to pin her down while he held her neck and head underwater. Her lungs and throat screamed for oxygen. Using every precious ounce of strength she could muster, she began beating him with her tiny fists, not knowing nor caring where her blows were landing. She was not going to die this way. She flat out refused. Just before she lost consciousness, she felt his grip loosen and his arms pull her up out of the water.

When she woke up, she saw she was in the boat and Erik was sitting on his bed, rocking back and forth. "Erik?" Her voice was extremely scratchy, and she could tell that there were deep bruises on her neck. At the sound of her voice, he approached her, and she saw that tears were streaming down his face. She could see tiny bruises on his face and arms where she had struck him. When he saw she was fully awake, however, he brushed his hand across his reddened face.

"My apologies for nearly killing you, Little Giry. Next time, it would be in your best interest to stay out of my way." His tone was not that of remorse. More like scolding. "I will give you the rest of the day to recover. Then I will see you back up to the dormitories."

"No you won't, because I'm not leaving you until I can be sure you won't harm yourself."

"It would be wise for you to rest your voice, brat. And you'll do as I say." With that, he turned and went back to his bed. Perhaps he was right. This recent outburst just went to show how very dangerous he could be. But then, would he be any less danger to himself, without her there to wake him from his nightmares? Oh, how she wished her mother was there right now. She would know exactly what to do. But she wasn't. All she knew was Erik needed her. His life depended on it.

Erik did not know whether he slept that night or not. All he remembered was suddenly being jolted back into reality when he smelled hot fish enter the room and felt a warm plate being placed on his lap. Her shuffling footsteps left him to his breakfast, but instead of hearing the creaking of the boat, he heard a scrubbing sound. *She couldn't possibly have recovered that much already!* He thought for sure she would be too weak today to protest him bringing her back to the surface world. But alas, she was there, seemingly skipping breakfast and throwing herself right into work. *So that's it, then. Trying to make me see how much I might need you? Well you won't fool me!* When she finished with the main floor, she stood to bring the bucket of water into the kitchen. He got a good look at her face then, and he saw that it was very pale, as if she was going to hurl any minute. Her steps were on wobbly legs, and she now grasped the bucket handle with her other hand to maintain her grip. All of a sudden, she let out a yelp and crashed to the floor. He would have applauded her performance, but it was then he saw her clutching her wrist, sobbing uncontrollably. This was way out of his comfort zone. "Let me see your wrist." He knelt down beside her, choosing to ignore the puddle of water from the dropped bucket. Slowly, she extended her hand, not looking up. He could see that it was already wrapped up, and wondered why he hadn't noticed it before. He cautiously undid the cloth, immediately noticing how swollen and purple it was. "How long has it been like this?" He demanded.

"Since that first night...when I found you...I...was stupid and I touched your shoulder...I...should have known better..." Meg was sobbing harder now.

"I did this?"

"It was my fault. I told you, I was stupid. You were on the brink of death and I..." Before she could finish, he picked her up and brought her to the lake. He set her down on the edge and dunked her hand into the cold water.

"Stay there. I'll be back." Mixed thoughts and opinions battled each other in his mind. On the one hand, he wanted to just ignore this and send her right up to Antoinette. On another hand, he knew that if he showed up with her daughter in the state she was in, he would be done for. So a third choice took over without him really deciding on it. Once before, he had sustained such an injury, upon building his traps. He had taken a bad fall through one of the steps, landing on his arm. Therefore, he knew what she needed. He grabbed a quite a few strips of cloth and four smooth pieces of scrap wood he had been saving for who-knows-what project. As soon as he felt her hand had soaked long enough, he gently dried it off and tied the wood around the injury to act as a splint. He then wrapped her whole hand up and placed it in the last cloth, tied into a sling.

"Thank you..." Her face was that of pure amazement, and it then hit him as to what he had just done. Had he, Erik/The Phantom/Opera Ghost...had he really just done something for someone other than himself?

"Yes...well...I expect you to be able to do your regular chores with just the one arm. As soon as you've recovered, I shall return you to your mother, and I'll hear no argument about it. I would just as soon return you today had I not made a certain promise to your mother." He didn't believe it. He would not believe it. He would not allow this side of himself to show to anyone. Anyone, except perhaps Christine. As he stormed back to his bed, he knocked the nearest candle stand into the water.

Meg knew better than to ask for the day off, no matter how sick she felt. At the tiniest complaint, she knew he would haul her back upstairs quicker than one could say "Phantom of the Opera." And so, dizzy and nauseous as she was, she made her way back to where the bucket lay on its side. Slowly, she picked it up and carried it down to the lake to refill it. Even slower, she hauled it back into the kitchen to work on that floor.

Erik jumped at the sound. Oh no. Not again. One good deed was enough for the day. But as it came to his ears over and over again, he let out an exasperated grunt and followed the sound into the kitchen. There she was, just barely above the floor, sobbing every time she caught her breath before a new wave came over her. He stood frozen for at least five minutes, having absolutely no idea as to what to do. Finally, he took notice of her long blond hair, now damp and stringy. Slowly, he knelt down and held her hair behind her back until it was all over. She then weakly turned around and placed her head on his chest, sobbing into his shirt. He almost yelled at her right then and there to quit soiling his clothes and to clean up the mess, but this feeling of having someone lean on him, to trust him enough in this hour of their weakness, well, it had never happened in his life. So he sat there, letting his arms wrap around her as she shook. For the first time in days, he was the strong one. She was relying on him now.

The thought scared him half to death. What was it like, to be needed? No one had ever needed him before, although he insisted that Christine had needed him, whether she admitted it or not. How else would she have gotten through those first few years of her grief if he had not been there, lending a song of comfort? He held Meg tighter then, forgetting that it was Meg and not Christine. The foul odor filling the room, however, snapped him back into reality. Carefully, he picked her up and carried her into the main room. At first he began to bring her to the boat, then stopped himself. If this was going to be his one day of good deeds, he might as well go all out and give her his bed. However, as he lowered her to the soft mattress, she clung to him as tight as her injury would allow. Well, what else could he do? He lowered himself to the bed beside her, and within the half hour, the dancer had fallen asleep next to him. His one arm was trapped under her sleeping form, and he dared not wake her. Instead, he turned his head away from her. *Why are you not Christine? Why?* Tears flooded down his face then, and he made no effort to stop them.

Chapter Six: Of Healings and Partings

It was the middle of the night when Meg woke up. It was not that she wasn't tired. She would have slept much longer had the image of her sobbing mother not suddenly appeared in her mind. Her stomach ached as well, both from hunger as well as sickness. She felt a lump under the back of her neck, and as she turned she saw that Erik was sleeping next to her. *Oh dear, Meg, you've really done it this time! Mama will surely lock you up for hundreds of years now!* But the more she gaped at the situation, the more innocent it became. Had she not been on top of his arm, he would most likely be on the other side of the cavern or at least fully turned away from her on his side. Meg let out a soft, tiny laugh at herself for worrying. *Well he can't be very comfortable. Why his arm is almost completely behind his back!* Slowly, Meg began to shift farther away from him on the bed, then felt his hand gently squeeze her shoulder as be began to wake up. "Can't sleep?" he mumbled.

"No, I...I didn't mean to wake you..."

"Do you feel like you need to...is it your stomach?" Panic rose in his voice.

"Well, it does hurt, but otherwise it's fine. I was just thinking of Mama, that's all."

"She's probably worried sick about you. What were you thinking, coming down here like you did? What did you expect to find?" He was now sitting up, fully awake.

Meg burst into tears all over again, and Erik inwardly groaned. *Now what did you have to go and do that for?* He gingerly put his hand on her shoulder, reluctant to get his arm trapped again. "I don't know! I honestly don't know! I know it sounds silly...stupid even. I've just had all these burning questions all these years...and I didn't know who else to turn to. Christine's been so preoccupied lately, and Mama..." Her words were now lost in her tears, and she leaned into his chest. Again. Erik sighed and, completely out of force of habit, began softly singing a song that had always made him feel better.

"Night-time sharpens, heightens each sensation ...

Darkness stirs and wakes imagination ... Silently the senses abandon their defenses ..."

No! Fool, what are you doing? That is no longer your song! It belongs to Christine! "You have such a lovely voice..." Meg commented sleepily.

"Don't get used to it. I sing only for Christine now." Erik let go of her shoulder and stood up.

"I'm sorry...I'm really sorry for everything, Erik. I'm sorry for bothering you...I'm sorry about Christine...I...I miss her too..." *How dare she!* Erik whirled around and stuck his face as close to hers as he could.

"Don't you ever, *ever*, say that! Don't you *dare* to even think that we share *anything*, especially Christine! You couldn't possibly know *anything* about my feelings for her!" Tears were flooding down her face, but Erik would not allow himself to care. He picked up a chair and flung it into the lake.

"Erik, I...I didn't mean it like that. I mean...maybe it's too soon for me to say this, but..."

"Then don't say it!"

"Oh but I must! I have to make this clear! Yes, I do miss Christine. She was like a sister to me all these years. We'd tell each other everything. And now...now she never talks to me. Sometimes it's because she's thinking of Raul...other times, I know she's thinking of you...she doesn't say it, of course, but it's in her eyes...she'll walk about as if she were still under your spell.

"And you, you miss her too! Not in the same way, of course, but you do miss her! Only with you it's harder because you know she's never coming back!"

"Enough! Enough!" Erik roared as he charged back over to her, raising his hand as if to strike. One look at her eyes, however, kept his hand at bay. Again. "Get back to sleep." He began walking away again, but then changed his mind. "In the boat." He watched as she slowly slid off his bed and stumbled on weakened legs over to the boat. As she lay down, he saw her glaring at him through a waterfall of tears. *Go ahead. Think me heartless. After all, that's who I am now. My heart was stolen and smashed by your precious friend Christine!* Erik collapsed onto his bed, voluntarily deafened to her sobs.

"Madame Giry, is Meg feeling any better today?" Madame Giry looked up from the spot on the floor she had been staring at. The question belonged to one of Meg's regular dance partners, Fredrique Dubois. The concern in his eyes almost caused Madame Giry to break down into sobs and let the whole truth out, but she composed herself.

"Not yet, Fredrique. I'm sorry."

"May I see her at least? I've been working on a new routine...I thought I might show it to her to cheer her up..."

"No, I'm sorry, Fredrique, but she will see no one. I won't have you catching anything either. Why don't you work on it a little more and show it to me later?" Fredrique nodded sadly and made his way down the hall.

"Madame Giry?" Christine had appeared behind her. "Meg's not really sick, is she?"

"I guess I can't fool you, Christine, can I? No she's not. At least I don't think so. Come with me." Antoinette led the soprano into her quarters and locked the door. "To be quite honest, my dear, I do not know where she is. She disappeared several days ago. I think she might be..."

"You think she's...with him?" Christine finished for her, and she simply nodded, tears reaching her eyes. "So, he couldn't have me so he grabbed the next best thing, is that it?"

"No, I don't think so, Christine. Meg has always been curious about him. I should have seen this coming. And now she's somewhere down there...and I don't know the way...it's so dark..." Pent up sobs were quickly taking over.

"Don't worry. Raul and I know how to get there. We'll take you there."

"And you, you're okay with this?"

"Meg's my best friend, Madame Giry. I'd do anything for her." Christine placed her hand on the ballet instructor's shoulder and smiled reassuringly. Inwardly, however, she was having second thoughts about facing her tormentor.

Meg woke up in a panic. The boat was moving! As her eyes adjusted, however, she saw that Erik was standing behind her, steering the boat with a long pole. "Erik, what's going on?"

"I'm taking you back upstairs, that's what's going on." Erik didn't look at her.

"I thought you were going to wait..."

"I don't care anymore. Your mother can do what she wants to me. I just don't care!"

What Meg did not know was that after they had both fallen asleep again, Erik's dream had been the most confusing and torturous one yet. As he steered the boat, the dream was still so fresh in his mind, he shuddered. *It was his wedding day. He watched*

Christine approach him, a smile on her face underneath the veil. The ceremony went on smoothly, and finally Erik lifted the veil and kissed his bride. As he pulled away, however, instead of Christine smiling into his eyes, the face was Meg's! Erik shuddered again, and began paddling faster.

"Oh, I should have known the boat would be gone!" Christine inwardly kicked herself as the three of them approached the rocky bank.

"Wait here. I'll go get her." Raul took his lantern and stepped into the freezing water.

"Be careful!" Madame Giry called out. Just as Raul was about to round the first corner, however, they heard the boat approaching.

Erik nearly jumped ten feet in the air at the sight of the intruders. Composing himself, he glared down at the young Vicomte who had now drawn his sword. "Put that away, boy, if you value your life!" Erik hissed.

"Erik, is Meg with you?" Antoinette called from the shore.

"Mama!" Meg nearly fell out of the boat in her excitement.

"Would you sit still and let me land this boat, woman?" Erik growled and regained control of the vessel. As soon as the boat touched land, Meg jumped out and ran into her mother's arms. "You'd best keep a better eye on your daughter, Antoinette. No telling what might happen to her if she comes down here again." It was then that Erik noticed Christine staring up at him, and he nearly collapsed. "Christine...you're...you came back..."

"Only for Meg. I see she is not returning unharmed." Christine turned her face away from him, pointing to Meg's bandaged arm.

"Oh, this? This is nothing, Christine...really all my fault. In fact, Erik was the one who bandaged it up for me. It's healing quite nicely thanks to him." Everyone turned to face Erik then, absolutely astonished.

"I...I uh...I didn't want...I wasn't..." For once, Erik was speechless.

"Thank you, Erik, for taking care of my daughter." Antoinette touched his shoulder, and he backed away.

"Come on, Meg. Let's get you back upstairs. Fredrique has been asking about you." Christine turned away from Erik and began walking away, Raul close behind.

"Christine, I..." Erik could feel tears returning to his eyes. *Must we say good bye again?*

"Good bye. I'll always be thankful for you teaching me all those years." Before he could respond, she and Raul were gone.

"Come, Meg." Antoinette began pulling her daughter toward the passageway.

"Wait...Erik, I can't leave without knowing for sure that you won't harm yourself." There were those eyes again.

"I'll make no such promise. This is my life, not yours. You'd be wise to mind your own business from now on."

"What if I just leave some bread and vegetables in the passageway? You won't have to see me, and you'll still get the food you need...fish can get pretty boring if you eat it every day..."

"I said I'll make no such promise! Now leave me!" Erik pushed the boat away then, refusing to say anymore good byes.

How did you find him, Meg? Was he very ill?" Madame Giry whispered as they followed Christine and Raul back through the tunnels and passageways.

"Oh, Mama, it was horrible! He hadn't eaten all that time! He was just lying there in his hiding spot...if I had gotten there any later, he would've..." Meg could not bring herself to think it.

"I am proud of you for sticking with him as he recovered, Meg. But you should not have gone down here all by yourself! Did I not warn you time and time again?" Meg hung her head, and her mother pulled her closer. "Ah, never mind. What's done is done. What matters is that you're safe."*But is Erik?* Meg couldn't help thinking.

Erik let the boat float in the middle of the lake. *If only I could grab that moment back...without Meg, without Antoinette, and most certainly without that insolent Vicomte! Just Christine and I...* "Oh, why, Christine? Why?"

After the worst of his sobbing fit was over, Erik guided the boat back to his living quarters. The foul stench coming from the kitchen cavern reminded him that he was once again on his own. *Well that's fine with me and good riddance! Who needs her, anyway?* He grabbed one of the rags Meg had used to scrub the floors and began erasing every single inch of her short existence in his home.

Chapter Seven: Adjusting

Over the next week and a half, Madame Giry maintained her story while Meg stayed in her bedchamber, allowing her wrist to fully heal. Upon removing the bandages once and for all, Meg carefully rolled them into a bundle and stored them in a box under her bed, a reminder of Erik's sweet side. She immediately set to work keeping up her end of the unofficial promise. Grabbing a basket from the prop room, she slowly made her way down to the kitchen. "Feeling better, Meg?" A somewhat familiar voice spoke from behind her. Meg jumped, then turned around.

"Fredrique! You startled me!"

"My apologies. I've been worried about you, you know. You've been sick for nearly a month."

"Yes, well...thank you for your concern. As you can see, I am much better now, so you need not worry anymore." To prove her point, she got up on her toes and twirled around.

"Then may I escort you back to the practice rooms? There's a new routine I've been working on that I'd like to show you."

"Oh, I'd love to see it, Fredrique, but..."

"Please. Call me Fred."

"Okay, Fred. Why don't you go warm up, and I'll meet you in there?" Disappointment filled his eyes, but he silently agreed. Meg hurried to fill the basket, bring it to the passageway behind Christine's dressing room mirror, and join her dance partner.

Erik threw the plate against the wall. *She was right. Curse you, Meg, for being right!* He had eaten one fish every day for the past week and a half, even though he had never promised to stay alive. He was avoiding sleep again, refusing to allow that image of Meg to enter his dreams again. Most of the time he sat on his bed, staring at the countless drawings of Christine and sobbing his eyes out. *Is this why you dragged me out of Death's grasp, Meg? So I can just sit here and think about her more? Curse you, curse you, curse you!* His growling stomach interrupted his thoughts, and he rolled his eyes. *Fine. I'll go up there, Meg, but you had better of left me something!* As he got into the boat, he caught a glimpse of a white object beside the seat, and as he picked it up, he saw it was his mask. *So, she had this all that time?* Realization hit him then. All that time Meg had been down here, not once had she shown fear of his face. *Just like her mother.* He began placing it onto his face, then flung it into the lake. *No! The Phantom is dead!* A look of determination, sorrow, and anger appeared on his face and stayed there as he made his way up to the passageway. Just as she had all but promised, a basket full of bread and vegetables sat behind the mirror, and he took a moment to peer into the dressing room. It was empty, and he didn't know whether to be relieved or disappointed. Finally, he picked up the basket and brought it back down into his cellars.

"**Oh, Fred, that was** wonderful!" Meg applauded from her chair. Fredrique bowed and then approached her.

"Now, Meg, allow me to show you another routine I've been working on. This one is for the two of us." He extended his hand, and as Meg took it, he led her to the center of the room. "Just follow my lead," he whispered. As they danced, Meg felt freer than she had ever felt before, and even though this was the first time she had danced this particular routine, she felt confident enough to close her eyes as her partner moved her around in spins, twirls, and leaps, until finally he threw her into the air, caught her, and lowered her to the floor in a beautiful finishing pose. "Meg, I always knew you learn quickly, but that was absolutely perfect." Fredrique whispered, trying to catch his breath.

"I should be the one complimenting you, Fred. You must have worked hard on that routine."

"Shall we go to supper now, Meg?" He helped her to her feet and extended his elbow.

"That sounds wonderful," Meg smiled.

Weeks turned into months, and soon the reconstruction was nearly complete. Everyone was soon throwing themselves into a production for the grand reopening, and Christine and Raul's wedding was planned for a month afterward. Meg soon found herself looking forward to seeing Fredrique, especially since Madame Giry had found a way to incorporate their dance into the production. Fredrique escorted Meg to supper almost every night, and although he had previously been fairly shy, he was soon gaining more confidence around her.

However, in the back of her mind, Meg still found herself worrying about Erik. Her basket of food had disappeared from behind the mirror, and so she knew he was still alive. *He'll be running out of food again soon, though.* She wondered how he was occupying himself during the day and if he was having anymore nightmares.

She was sitting on her dorm bed one afternoon, pondering this very thing as she ran a comb through her long blond hair. One of the other dancers entered then, and handed her a plain white envelope. "Thank you, Alyce," Meg took it gratefully. Inside was a note, apparently from Christine.

"Meg,

Come see me in my old dressing room. There's something we need to discuss regarding my wedding. I'll be in there at 4 o' clock.

~Christine"

"What time is it now, Alyce?" Meg asked.

"Fifteen minutes 'til four," Alyce replied.

"Thank you. Tell Mama that I will be ready to practice in about one hour." Meg watched as the younger dancer left the room, then finished with her hair, putting it into braids. She then made her way down the hall and into the dressing room.

Erik scowled at the once-again empty kitchen. He had two options. One was to go back to eating nothing but fish, and the other was to admit his reliance on Meg once again. The thought of the dry, bony fish meat entering his mouth day after day made up his mind for him. He guided the boat back through the lake, now littered with masks, wigs, and costumes that he had dumped in his killing off of his alter-ego. As he made his way toward the passageways, he felt his head spinning from lack of sleep and various bouts of rage. He pushed on, however, feeling that a full stomach would make him feel much better.

When he approached the spot behind the mirror, he frowned when he saw it was empty. Voices from the dressing room stopped him from roaring in frustration, and he ducked into the shadows where he could see in, but no one could see him. He recognized Meg right off, and there was a look of confusion on her face.

"Fred? What are you doing here?" Meg had just barely sat down on Christine's floral sofa when the boy dancer entered the room, locking the door behind him.

"I see you got my note, my beautiful dancer."

"*Your* note? Then why did you use Christine's name?"

"I...I wasn't sure if you would come if you knew it was me."

"Oh, Fred, of course I would have. Really, you undervalue yourself." Meg placed a reassuring hand on his arm, and finally his look of concern turned into a smile. "Now tell me, what is this about? And why here?"

"I chose this place because I was trying to think like Christine."

"That does make sense. Now come, what is it? A new routine, perhaps?"

"You might say that." Fredrique took her hands and walked her to the center of the room.

"Is this room big enough?" Meg questioned, doubt in her voice.

"Yes, it's adequate enough." A new look came over his face then...one of hunger. Before she could say anything, he covered her mouth with his. Meg pulled her face away.

"No, Fred...control yourself!" He shoved her to the floor then, pinning her arms over her head.

"If you value your mother's life, Marguerite, you'll not breathe a word of this to anyone." Fredrique hissed before roughly kissing her again. He then used his full weight to hold her down as he moved his hands across her chest and down toward her hips. Meg closed her eyes, tears streaming out of the corners as she tried once more to struggle. Her attempt was met with a sharp blow to her face, and she felt her skirts being lifted up. Just as she was about to completely give up, she felt him being thrown off of her. She opened her eyes in time to see Erik kneeling down beside her, and Fredrique was just getting up off of the floor. He hurriedly unlocked the door and ran out into the hallway.

"Meg, are you all right?" Erik asked, concern filling his face and his voice. Before Meg could reply, the door was flung open as Fredrique, Madame Giry, Christine, and Alyce rushed into the room.

"Erik, what do you think you are doing?" Madame Giry all but screeched. Erik backed away, arms in the air.

"No, Mama, you don't understand! Erik did nothing but save my life!" Meg protested. Fredrique threw a glare in her direction, and as soon as he saw she had seen him, he subtly showed a dagger hidden in his belt, then pointed to Madame Giry with a raised eyebrow and a smirk.

"Don't try to protect him, Meg. Fredrique tells me he heard you scream, and he came running. He saw him on top of you, and he quickly came to get me." Madame Giry replied.

"Yes, and Alyce said that she delivered a note signed in my name to you." Christine spoke up.

"Well, Erik? What do you have to say for yourself?"

Erik had seen Fredrique's motions aimed at Meg, and he quickly understood. "Mama, please, you have to believe me..." Meg began.

"No, Meg. It's no use. I'll not bother you again. It's...for the best." Erik stood then, and before Meg could even think of protesting, he had disappeared down the tunnel. *So much for good deeds! Well, Monsieur Fredrique, you had better think twice of going anywhere alone for a while! How dare he threaten Antoinette and Meg!* As he guided his boat back to his living quarters, he dug angrily into the water. *The insolent fool! Now Christine will NEVER love me!*

"**You're letting him** go? Well I say, let's follow that monster before he tries this again!" Fredrique drew his dagger and started for the mirror.

"No, Fred. He'll not harm us again." Madame Giry grabbed his shoulder.

"He better be sure he doesn't! In the meantime, Meg, might I offer my services to guard you?"

"That won't be necessary." Meg glared at him.

"If you'll all excuse us, I'll see that Meg gets fixed up for supper." Christine went over to her friend, pulling her into a hug. As soon as the door was closed, Christine gently led Meg to the sofa, handing her a handkerchief.

"Christine, you believe me, don't you?" Meg looked at her pleadingly.

"Shush, Meg. You mustn't say such things about the Phantom. Before you know it, he'll have you under his spell, and it'll be near impossible for you to escape him."

"His name is Erik. And he's a better man than you think. Do you not remember that it was he who fixed up my arm?"

"Please, Meg, don't be naive. You forget he won me over by teaching me how to sing and arranging for me to get the lead in all those productions. One arm is nothing compared to that." Christine brushed the tears off of Meg's face. "Let's not think about it anymore. Here, you may take your pick of any of my dresses."

Chapter Eight: A Plan

All too soon, it was the final rehearsal before the grand reopening of the Opera Populaire. Meg stood anxiously off stage, dreading her cue. Carlotta was in the middle of her solo, and then it would be time for the dance. Before she saw Fredrique approach her, she felt his cold hands slide around her waist. "Ready, my lovely dancer?" He smirked down at her.

"No." Meg looked away from him as he let out a laugh.

"Too late to back out now, Marguerite. Carlotta is finishing." Meg watched as Carlotta flashed one of her wide grins at the empty house before marching toward her posse to run through her list of complaints. Fredrique half dragged Meg onstage as their music began, and Meg went through the routine emotionlessly and stiffly. At the finish, Fredrique pulled her into an empty corner backstage. "What were you doing out there? Where's that fire you've had?"

"Where do you think?" Meg spat at him.

"Well be sure that it's back tonight, or else!" Fredrique showed her his dagger again before storming off. Meg looked up, tears starting to stream down her face. Her mother was looking at her as if to say "I'm sorry, but he's right." *Oh, Mama, if only I could tell you!* Instead, she brushed the tears off her face and prepared for the next dance number.

That night, as Fredrique pulled her onto the stage to face half of Paris, he threw her a warning look as the music began. Taking a deep breath, Meg danced with as much passion as she had hatred toward her partner, and it seemed to work, for they were met with a standing ovation. "That's my girl." Fredrique sneered at her, but she ignored him.

When the opera was over, Meg decided to not join the rest of the cast at the backstage celebration. Instead, she ran sobbing into the kitchen, grabbed a loaf of bread and a few vegetables, and then made her way back toward Christine's room and the passageway. There was no boat, of course, to meet her at the lake, but she did not care. Raising the food above her head, she waded through waste deep water until the sight of candle light welcomed her. "Erik!" she cried.

Erik rushed out of the kitchen, where he had been unwillingly fishing. He watched Meg emerge from the lake, shivering and sobbing. "What on earth are you thinking, woman?" He grabbed the food from her and threw it on the bed before wrapping a blanket around her soaked legs.

"Teach me to sing."

"What?"

"Teach me to sing. I refuse to dance anymore with that...that..." Erik sat her down on one of his chairs and knelt down beside her.

"Calm down, Meg, and think about this. Firstly, I told you already that I do not sing anymore. My music was my heart, and Christine will always have that. Secondly, if your mother finds you down here again, you know what she'll do to me!"

"I don't care! I refuse to look at him, Erik! I refuse to allow him to look at me with those greedy eyes and those taunting smirks! You're the only one I can turn to now! I can't tell anyone else, or he'll..."

"I know, Meg. Why do you think I didn't defend myself against his lies? Your mother helped me in my greatest time of need, and so I care a great deal about her welfare. And I came to your rescue because..."

"There's no need to explain that, Erik."

"Yes there is, because I don't want you to misinterpret my actions. I did it because I thought...if Christine saw me helping you, she might look at me differently...not like a monster..."

"Oh, Erik...when will you let her go? When will you realize that she..."

"Don't say it, Meg! Don't even think it!" Erik forced her chin up so that she could look him in the face. As he looked into her eyes, he saw disappointment and sadness, and he turned away. "As soon as you've dried off, I'll take you back."

"No! Don't you understand? I cannot...I will not face that man again!"

"So you're just going to give up and let him win? Suppose you do stay down here and give up dancing. Your mother will come looking for you and start asking questions. You'll eventually break down and tell her, and Fredrique will follow through on his threats."

"If I stay up there, she'll notice my lack of interest and ask questions anyway!"

"Meg, please. Go back upstairs before you're missed. Spend the night thinking things through. If it would make you feel better, I do have a tunnel behind the walls of your dorm room. I just never use it because of a certain promise I made to your mother. If you'd like, I'll spend the night there, keeping an eye out for him. Can you at least agree on that?"

"And if I don't change my mind?"

"We'll cross that bridge if we come to it." Oh, he had a plan alright, but it was not one he wanted to tell to Meg. It consisted of hunting down Fredrique and slipping a rope around his neck, and then Meg would be free to tell the truth. Then, Christine would finally see and come back to him. Meg would go back to her dancing and finally leave him alone.

"I suppose I can agree to that, Erik. And I want to thank you for saving my life. If you hadn't been there..."

"Don't think about it. Dry your tears while I fix my supper, and then we'll be off." Erik grabbed a small piece of bread and a carrot, then at the last minute he groaned and sliced off a piece of the fish, quickly frying it. Upon his return, Meg was standing up and placing the blanket on his chair. She let a few sniffles escape, but she smiled bravely at him and got into the boat.

"What's with all the masks in the water?"

"That part of me has died off. Do not speak of 'the Phantom' again." The rest of the journey was silent, and he led her back to the mirror. "Go on. I promise I'll be right there, watching out for him." Meg took his hand and squeezed it before stepping through, and he waited until the door had closed before continuing on through the tunnel. He stopped in front of what appeared to be a dead end, but he pulled down the curtain and pressed one of the stones, revealing an abandoned set of tunnels. He only hoped that he could remember which way led to Meg's room.

"Meg where have you been? Fredrique has been looking for you!" Madame Giry exclaimed. *I'll bet he has,* Meg though bitterly.

"Mama, if you don't mind, I wish to retire early. This has been such a long day."

"Well, all right, dear. I'll pass your regrets on. Good night." Meg made her way to her dorm room, relieved to see it empty. She slowly crept to the back wall.

"Erik? Are you there?" She whispered.

"Mademoiselle, you should know that when I give my word, I do not break it. Now silence!" She heard him hiss, and she had to suppress a giggle.

"Good night, then, Monsieur." She tiptoed back to her bed, too tired to change into her night clothes. *Besides, for all I know he can see me right now!* At that thought, she quickly buried herself under her blankets.

As Erik nibbled his bread and fish, he watched through a tiny gap in the stone wall as Meg tossed and turned throughout the night. *She's not going to change her mind. I just know it.* As he thought over his plan, however, he realized that he could never go through with it if he wanted to win over Christine. He remembered that she hated murder, even if it was for her sake. He recalled that dawn in the graveyard. Even though Raul was clearly trying to protect her, she refused to allow him to finish Erik off. And then there was the kiss...the kiss that should have told him that she was only going along with it to prevent Raul's death. But no, he refused to let that thought in all its truth to sink in. As long as he kept the tiniest glimmer of hope, there was still a chance.

Meg feigned sleep until the last of the dancers had left the room the next morning. Slowly, she crept back to the wall where she knew Erik was hiding. "Erik, I want you to know that I haven't changed my mind."

"I didn't expect that you would, although it would be a lie to say I'm not disappointed."

"Do you have a plan then?"

"I do. We'll let your mother catch him red-handed. During breakfast, I want you to persuade your mother and Christine to join you in here. Instead of flat-out inviting Fredrique, I want you to act suspicious enough so that he will follow you. Once you are all in here, tell the truth. I'll take care of the rest."

"You want me to risk the life of my mother?"

"Trust me, Meg. This is the only way."

"I...I trust you."

"Then you'd better change. Don't worry, I'll look away."

As Meg carried out her part of the plan, she was positive her heart was beating so hard that it was causing the rest of her body to shake. She made sure Fredrique saw her whisper nervously to her mother and to Christine, and after the meal was finished, she caught a glimpse of him standing up as they left the room. *Oh, Erik, you'd better be right about this!*

"All right, Meg, now what is this about?" Madame Giry closed the door as they entered the dorm room.

"Is it about your sudden lack of interest in dancing?" Christine guessed.

"Yes it is actually. That afternoon, when I was...attacked...I didn't tell you everything. It wasn't Erik that attacked me, I told you that much. What I didn't tell you is that my attacker was Fred-"

"I'll teach you to heed my warnings, little dancing brat!" The door was kicked open, and in one swift move, Fredrique drew his dagger, crossed the room, and grabbed the ballet instructor from behind her neck. Before he could dig the blade into Madame Giry, the back wall opened up, and Erik rushed into the room, grabbed the dagger from the stunned youth, and pinned him to the side wall.

"Listen here, Monsieur Fredrique, and listen good. If you ever...*ever* even *think* about threatening Madame Antoinette or her daughter *ever again*, I will spill every single drop of your cowardly blood on this floor with no hesitation. Do I make myself clear?"

"Clear as...glass..."

"Good. Now pack your bags and leave this opera house. Now!" Erik flung the dancer towards the door, smirking as he disappeared without the tiniest glance back.

"Do you believe me now, Mama?" Meg's mousy voice broke the silence, and Madame Giry pulled her into a tight, tearful embrace.

"Oh, Meg, I'm so sorry, my dear!" By now, mother and daughter were sitting on the nearest bed, sobbing into each other. Christine stood in her place, staring at Erik as if she were in a trance and about to faint.

"So, Christine, there's a lot more to me than you think. I'm not all bad, you know. At least, you would know, if you'll open your heart to me."

"No..please...don't do this to me again! Just what do I have to do to make you see that I love Raul?" Christine emerged from her trance as tears began to flow.

"I'll admit that you do care for him, my dear. But don't be so quick to forget that we share something much deeper. All those nights of singing to each other...your voice becoming stronger as my music became yours..."

"Stop it, Erik! Stop it right this instant!" Madame Giry cut in. "Am I to understand that this was all to impress Christine? Meg and myself were merely pawns in this scheme of yours?"

"No..I mean...I do care about you, Antoinette, and would stop at nothing to see that you remain unharmed. But..."

"But you still have feelings for Christine."

"Erik, you need to let her go. In less than a month, Christine will marry the Vicomte. They will begin their future together elsewhere. You need to let them go and think about your own life." Meg stood up and planted herself between Erik and Christine. "I know you don't want to hear this, but you've got to. You need to face reality." Before Erik could shush her, she turned to face Christine. "As for you, Christine, while I wish you and Raul all the happiness in the world, there is one more thing you need to do before the wedding. You must stop hating Erik. All he did was love you. Is that such an awful crime? Perhaps he went about it the wrong way, but if you'd have spent as much time down in his caverns as long as I have, you'd understand how isolated he really is from the world and all its rules and formalities. You mustn't leave here with this hatred in your heart. It will destroy you sooner or later."

"Meg, why are you still defending him? He used you! He used us all!"

"Don't speak to me as if I were a naive child. I know what he did, and I'll pass my own judgment. But Christine, you didn't see him when I found him. You didn't see him feverish, cold, and hungry, and still sobbing for you. Try to at least attempt to understand his point of view. Don't misunderstand me, dear friend. I know that you and Raul belong together. I just want you to show a little more consideration and understanding."

"My dear, you are wise beyond your years." Madame Giry spoke up.

"I don't know, Meg. I just don't know. I don't think I can...it's not as easy as you think."

"There's no need, Christine. I see now that you'll never love me. Forget me." With that, Erik turned and disappeared through the hidden doorway, shutting it behind him.

Chapter Nine: A Friendship is Born

Meg spent the remainder of the day with Madame Giry and Christine, looking after the younger dancers while giving each other glances of reassuring comfort whenever they could. As the evening drew nearer, however, Meg took the first opportunity she could to sneak back down to Erik's cellars, this time well prepared for the cold water and dressed in her 'Don Juan' trousers. As she approached his home, she saw him placing various items into a satchel on his bed. "Leaving, Monsieur?" He jumped at the sound of her voice, a clear indication as to how troubling his thoughts were. Surely he would have heard her splashing through the water otherwise.

"There's nothing to keep me here." He only gave her a fleeting glance and continued packing. Silently, Meg made her way towards his beautiful organ and picked up the violin that was kept beside it.

"Don't forget this." She held it out to him. He looked down at it, backing away as if it were poison, and yet she could see in his eyes that he longed to play it. "Erik, it's time. You need this."

"No...I...I can't. Without Christine, I wouldn't know what to play."

"Erik, if I can go back to dancing, surely you can go back to your music. You need it just as much as I need dancing."

"It's not the same! You still have something to dance for. I have nothing!" Erik roughly latched the satchel and, turning his back to her, he stood facing the kitchen doorway. Silence fell over them and lasted for five minutes. "I notice you're not trying to stop me from leaving."

"What can I say, Erik? I've said all I can, and you've clearly made up your mind." Meg tried halfheartedly to block her tears. Finally, she moved past him into the kitchen and gathered up his food into the basket he hadn't returned. Turning back to face him, she extended the basket to him. When he grasped the handle, she held on. "No, I can't stop you from leaving, Erik. Just please...don't leave like this. Don't leave all these issues unresolved."

"What have I told you about minding your own business?" Erik grabbed the basket out of her hand and picked up the satchel.

"That's just it, Erik, this is my business now! You say there's nothing to keep you here when there are two people who deeply care about you and would be worried sick about you if you left. You just don't see that because you're always going to be focused on Christine! No matter how far you go from here, you're always going to be thinking about her and torturing yourself with this! You can't run away from your problems! You have to face them!"

"It's time you and your mother learned not to care so much. It only leads to heartache." With not one word of good bye, Erik turned and disappeared past the curtain and into the tunnel where she had initially found him. Meg desperately looked around for anything that might change his mind. Finally she saw that he had left the monkey toy, and she hurriedly wound it up, letting it play right outside of the tunnel. As soon as the music slowed to a stop, the curtain was shoved aside, and Erik's face appeared once more, covered in tears. "So you drag me back once more into the land of the living. Why do you care so much?"

"You forget, Erik. My mother is Madame Antoinette Giry." Meg forced a smile through her tears, and he chuckled with her. "Erik, I'll make a deal with you. If you promise to stay, I'll promise to keep talking to Christine until she agrees to make amends with you. What do you say?"

"I'll give you until the day before her wedding. If she doesn't speak to me by then, I'll not burden this opera house anymore."

"Trust me, Erik. It won't come to that because she will speak to you. In the meantime, at least try to return to your music. You'll go mad without it. Besides...I never told anyone this, but some nights, when I couldn't sleep, I would hear the faintest violin music coming through the vents. It was the most beautiful thing I've ever heard, and it always lulled me to sleep. If I knew that I was never going to hear that again, it would be the saddest thing I'd ever known."

"Oh, don't be so dramatic." Erik sighed. "I'll try. It won't be easy, but I'll try."

"Thank you. I should return now, before I miss curfew."

"I'll see you across the lake. You know the way from there."

So, the little dancer could hear me all that time. I should take better care of when I play from now on...if I play anything at all... Erik thought to himself as he guided the boat back. He could not let the scowl linger, however, as Meg's words played through his mind. "...There are two people who deeply care about you..." she had said. *She's right, you know. If you'd just take off those blinders...*

"What if I'm not ready to take them off? What if I don't want to see it?"

Then you'll die a stubborn old man, all alone in your dark, cold cave. You'll have pushed everyone who cares about you away, and Christine even further, and so no one would be left to care as to whether you live or die, is that what you want?

"Silence yourself!"

So not only do you choose to be blind, you also choose to be deaf. No wonder you can't go back to your music.

"Enough!" Erik roared, then realized no one was there. It had been his own thoughts and feelings he had been arguing with, which frustrated him even more.

Before he knew it, he was back in his living quarters, and he slowly walked to where the violin was sitting on his table. Part of him wanted to throw it into the lake to join his former alter-ego, but the majority of him stopped himself. No, the violin was far too valuable, as was all the rest of his instruments and music sheets. Slowly, he picked it up and found the bow. Sitting down, he moved it into position and slid the bow across the strings. A single note sang out, penetrating his hardened soul and bringing him back to the pure joy of creating music. Like a thirsty wanderer in a desert oasis, he played some more, drinking in the music until his stomach hurt, and finally he lowered the violin to the floor, put his head in his hands, and wept for the remainder of the night.

Meg smiled from her bed. *He was playing again.* When she heard the music fade away, she heard a much fainter sound of his sobbing. *I'm proud of you, Erik,* she thought as she succumbed to sleep once more.

Erik paced the cave floor anxiously. Three weeks had passed since Meg had talked him into making that deal, and still no word had reached him. *She'll never convince Christine. I just know it. I'm just wasting my time. I should never have listened to that little ballet dancer!* He clenched his fists and crossed the floor to where his violin sat. He picked it up, then set it right back down again. *How can I possibly focus on music now? This isn't working, Meg! I've changed my mind!* But seeing as Meg couldn't possibly hear his thoughts from up in the opera house, he was forced to stick to his word. *A promise is a promise, I suppose...* Erik sighed. Finally, he decided to occupy his mind with preparing his supper.

Oh, Erik of little faith, for while he was pacing the floor like a caged lion, Meg was using all her stubborn, sweet, patient logic to work her way past Christine's defenses. Finally, after three weeks of hearing nothing but Erik this and Erik that, Christine threw up her hands and permitted Meg to send a message down to Erik's caverns.

"*Erik,*

I hope you realize that your life has been saved by none other than the Angel of Logic. Who can argue with her when all she speaks is the truth! After much thought, I have decided that I will agree to settle things. In two days, I will meet with you in Madame Giry's quarters. I will only agree to this if you will allow Raul, Meg, and Madame Giry to be present as well. Please send word with Meg as soon as she delivers this. And I hope that when we do meet, you will be open to listening as much as you are open to speaking your mind. We will be looking for you at noon.

Until then,

Christine"

"Well it certainly took you long enough," Erik spoke gruffly as he set the note down.

"Don't complain. I held up my end of the bargain."

"You may tell Christine that I will allow everyone to be present, as long as the Vicomte agrees to no weapons. If I'm to show them that they can trust me, I expect no less from them."

"Fair enough. Now am I to swim back or can you drag yourself away from your pacing long enough to bring me back in your boat?"

"Difficult, insolent nuisance of a girl!" Erik mumbled under his breath as he stepped into the boat. "Are you coming or not?" Meg giggled at his impatience and took her seat. As soon as they were at the foot of the stairs, she got out, turned around, and curtsied.

"See you in two days, Monsieur! And thank you for the ride!" Erik watched as she cheerfully bounced up the stairs, and once she disappeared, he chuckled to himself, shaking his head.

Chapter Ten: Letting Go

Erik took a deep breath before entering Madame Giry's private quarters. They were most definitely asking a lot of him by holding the meeting here, as he hadn't built a passageway here. To have done so would have broken the bond of trust between the two friends. So he had spent a good half hour creeping through Meg's dorm room, down the hall, and to this very spot, making sure to remain unseen. Slowly, he turned the door knob, and as the door swung open, four pairs of eyes turned to meet his. "You're late." Meg was the first to dare to speak. Of course.

"No, Mademoiselle, I happen to be right on time. You are just early." Erik closed the door and stood awkwardly away from them.

"Please sit down, Erik, before you cause this room to shrink into nothing before our very eyes!" Antoinette smiled, and Erik slid into the closest chair to the door.

"Hello, Erik." Christine spoke up, and he slowly turned to face her, greeting her with a nod. He didn't dare to speak or even think. "I suppose I'll start, since it appears that you are unable to speak at the moment..." *Oh just get on with it!* Erik silently pleaded, trying unsuccessfully to not stare at her. "Ten years ago, I came to this opera house an orphan, filled with sorrow and pain. While Madame Giry and Meg welcomed me with warmth and kindness, there was still a piece missing. When my father was still around, the house was always filled with such beautiful music and singing...I sincerely thought my life was perfect. Then he died, and I thought...I thought I could never sing again. Not without him there. I don't know how many times I slipped into the chapel to light a candle for him, just in one day alone! Then you came, Erik. You heard me when I was crying out and saying things I never would have said had I known anyone on Earth was listening. Erik, you gave me back my voice, and I never got around to thanking you properly. In fact, I betrayed you. Oh, Raoul, get that look out of your face! I really do love you!" Christine turned back to Erik. "Erik, I think you will understand this most of all...when Raoul came back, I was so blinded by my love for him that I didn't think about the pain I might cause anyone. While you did things that were wrong and really frightening, I should not have pushed you away so harshly...I should not have pulled off your mask in front of all those people. I...I'm sorry, Erik."

Erik sat frozen in his seat, too astonished to even let the tears stinging his eyes fall down his cheeks. He didn't trust himself enough to speak, and yet everyone was watching him, waiting for him to say something. Anything. "I...I should be the one saying sorry, Christine. Not you. I can see that you really have been doing some thinking about this."

"Meg helped quite a bit. I can't take all the credit." Christine pointed out.

"Yes, well...I must admit, I hadn't thought about comparing your actions with my own. But I see now that that's exactly what happened. We were both blinded. It would be an understatement to say I spent almost all my life completely alone. Madame Giry was my only friend through most of it. When you came to the opera house, and when I heard you in the chapel, my only thoughts were that finally there was someone to share in my loneliness. Finally someone would know how I feel. From that day on, that is what guided me. The idea of sharing my life, my music with someone who would understand. I was wrong to deceive you from the start. I was wrong to try to tear you away from all you love and care about just to fulfill my selfish longings. I must confess that I still care very deeply for you, Christine, but you have my word as a gentleman that I will never again stand between you and your true love. I thought for sure that I would never be able to play or sing another note without you, but Meg here has shown me that I do still have a bit of music left in me. I can't say that it will happen instantly, but I am trying, I really am. I'm asking now if we might start over as friends?"

"That sounds wonderful. I would be honored to call you my friend, Erik." Christine smiled at him.

"There's just one thing, Erik. You are still a wanted man for the murders of Joseph Buquet and Piangi and the burning down of this opera house. Now, I'm not saying that I'd be the one to turn you over to the authorities, but surely the managers and Carlotta would say otherwise." Raoul spoke up. Erik winced at the mere mention of the Prima Dona's name.

"I believe Erik has already paid his debt for the destruction he caused to this building. As for the other charges...perhaps you and I could work something out with the managers and Carlotta tomorrow." Antoinette responded for him.

"When you do meet with them, I suppose you might mention to Carlotta that I promise not to interfere with her voice. I'll simply move to the other side of the world." Erik smirked, and they all laughed.

"Now, Erik, as a personal friend of both Raoul and myself, I would be honored if you would grace us with your presence at our wedding next week." Christine invited.

"Exactly how many other guests will be present?" Erik cringed.

"Oh, dear...I hadn't thought of that...perhaps one of your masks?" Erik let out a loud groan and slumped to the floor. "Was it something I said?" Christine asked worriedly.

"I may have failed to mention that all of Erik's masks are currently littering the bottom of his lake." Meg bit her lower lip sheepishly.

"Never mind. I'm sure that we'll think of something. This is an opera house, is it not? There's plenty of costuming and make up." Antoinette reminded them. At that, Erik breathed a sigh of relief.

"Yes, Christine, I will be there to share in your joyous event." He stood up and bowed formally.

"In fact, Erik, and this might be asking far too much of you, but I've been doing some thinking in regards to walking down the aisle. I have no family, as you know...and since I see you as a teacher and father figure, would you mind...being the one to give me away?"

"Christine, I don't think..." Raoul began.

"I'd be honored." Erik interrupted.

"Erik, are you sure you're ready?" Antoinette's voice was filled with doubt.

"I would not have agreed if I was not ready. Besides, it's the least I can do for my best pupil." Erik smiled.

"Silly. I'm your only pupil." Christine grinned.

"Oh, I don't know. I might just be considering taking on another student." Erik hinted teasingly.

The day of the wedding was soon upon them, and as the guests were flooding into the cathedral, Erik paced the floor outside the sanctuary. A last minute change to the wedding plans called for everyone in the wedding party to wear a decorative mask, and they had found an extra one in the prop room for Erik to wear. He had also borrowed a wig, but after going without one for so long, he was soon very uncomfortable with it. "Are you ready, Erik?" Meg's voice called out, and he turned to face the maid of honor. Her dress was of dark green silk, elegant in its simplicity. Her mask was also dark green with feathers all around the top.

"I'm as ready as I'll ever be. Might I say that you look lovely, Mademoiselle."

"Why thank you, good Monsieur." Meg curtsied. The rest of the bridal party joined them then, and once they had lined up, the doors opened and the processional began. As Meg began walking, Erik watched Christine slowly join him from the dressing room. He tried not to stare at how beautiful she looked, and so he chose to stare at the floor as she took his arm.

"Thank you for doing this, Erik. It means a lot to me." Christine whispered.

"It is my pleasure. You look beautiful, Christine. Raoul's a lucky man." Erik swallowed the lump in his throat and gave her a half smile. The wedding march began then, and Erik was forced to focus his attention to the front of the sanctuary, where Raoul stood. Erik watched the groom's face as he took in the image of his bride, and he quickly glanced at Christine. She, too, had that same look on her face, and Erik inwardly nodded to himself. Yes, he was ready to do this. Taking a deep breath, he escorted Christine down the flower petal-covered aisle and toward her future. Once in front of the priest, Erik placed Christine's hand into Raoul's before joining Antoinette in her pew. Watching the ceremony continue, he could not help but smile. Surely, these two belonged together. He could see it now, and fully accept it. *I just feel so lonely still. Is there no one for me?*

Chapter Eleven: A New Pupil

"May I have this dance, Mademoiselle Giry?" Erik extended his hand to Meg, who was sitting alone at the wedding table.

"Why, certainly, Monsieur." Meg allowed him to lead her to the center of the room, where the majority of the guests were dancing. "To be quite honest, I did not know you could dance." She commented as the music began again.

"I've observed enough from behind the opera house walls to have learned a step or two. Have you forgotten that I was at the New Year's masquerade?"

"Oh, yes, you do have a point. Dear me, that seems so long ago..."

"Yes, a lot has changed since then." Erik seemed lost in thought as they twirled around the room. "Meg, I have a confession to make."

"Oh?"

"There is a reason I asked you for this dance. Remember when I told Christine that I was thinking of taking on another pupil?"

"Yes. I assumed you were joking at the time."

"I meant for it to sound as though I was, in case you are no longer interested...you have gone back to dancing, of course. From the glimpses I've seen of your talent, I must say that you were born to do it, and I hope you keep that as your top priority. However, if you are still interested in working on your voice, I would be happy to teach you. It seems my future is a blank page now."

"Well, a few lessons couldn't hurt. In fact, from what I've seen in Christine, I know that you will be a great tutor."

"Then it is settled. I will need to spend some time with my music first, as soon as I hear a sample of your voice. Once I hear you sing, it will give me what I need to compose your songs."

"My songs?"

"Yes...I wrote songs to fit Christine's voice, and so I'll need to write songs for yours."

"I see." The song stopped just then, and the two clapped for the band before politely going their separate ways. For Erik, this meant politely asking Antoinette for a dance. For Meg, it meant going back to her seat, all alone. Erik caught frequent glances of her from over Antoinette's shoulder, and a small part of him recognized that bored expression on her face from the night of the masquerade. Of course, at the time, all his attention had been on Christine, but he had noticed her. At the end of the song, he thanked Antoinette for the dance and approached Meg once more.

"You look bored, Mademoiselle. Are you not happy for the newlyweds?"

"Of course I am. I'm just a bit tired is all." Meg threw him a *how dare you* look.

"Yes, it is getting quite late. Do you mind if I join you?" Meg replied by gesturing to the seat next to her, and he sat down. Just then, Carlotta got up and spoke to the conductor, who immediately stopped the music. "Oh dear me, what on earth is she doing now?" Erik groaned.

"'Allo everyone! It seems I have been asked to perform a song for the 'appy couple! And so, my gift to you, Vicomte and Vicomtess de Chagney!"

"Oh please, she's not fooling anyone with that smile. We all know she's jealous of them..." Meg mumbled under her breath.

"Could it be that sweet little innocent Marguerite has just spoken ill of someone?" Erik feigned shock.

"You weren't supposed to hear that." Meg flushed. "Oh, perhaps there is a slight chance that she has changed her attitude toward them, now that she's back as the lead soprano...but I rather doubt it." Before Erik could respond, Carlotta screeched out an especially high note, and Erik had to practically sit on his hands to keep from covering his ears. As the song progressed, Erik found himself squinting, ducking, and gritting his teeth at every missed pitch, which was practically every other note. Just when he thought he couldn't take it any longer, the song ended, and he was forced to join in on the applause.

"Please tell me that was the only one she's going to sing!" He muttered to Meg.

"Perhaps after you're done teaching me, she could be your next pupil?" Meg grinned.

"My dear girl, there's no one who can help that!" Erik whispered back. Thankfully, no one yelled for an encore, and it was announced that Christine was ready to toss the bouquet. Meg hurriedly joined the other single woman at the bottom of the stairs, and Erik watched as the red and white roses flew through the air, landing smoothly in Meg's outstretched hands. She triumphantly made her way back to the table, showing off the flowers. "Good catch." Erik smiled.

"Are you ready to go, Marguerite?" Antoinette joined them. "This is our last chance to bid the newlyweds good bye."

"Yes, I'm ready Mama." Meg yawned, and Erik stood. He helped them both with their cloaks before they went outside to see the couple off. He waited until they had both given their hugs, then shook hands with Raoul.

"Take good care of her, Raoul, as I know you are capable of." He spoke with politeness, but the look in his eyes showed how serious he was.

"I will, Erik. Thank you." Raoul nodded reassuringly, and Erik moved on to Christine.

"No matter what life brings, Christine, never stop singing. I won't be there to give you back your voice the next time life doesn't go your way. I wish you both all the happiness in the world. You deserve it." He grasped her hand and gave it a gentle squeeze, then let it go.

"Thank you, Erik. For everything."

"Take care!" Erik waved to them before turning to join Antoinette and Meg as they walked to their own carriage. He helped them in before taking his own seat next to Antoinette. As they pulled away, he could feel that familiar ache and longing return to his heart, but this time he knew it was not for love lost, rather for knowing that he was bound to face his life alone. Again.

"Well, what should I sing?" Meg bit her lip. It was two days later, and she was standing next to his organ bench.

"Anything that shows off your full vocal range." Erik replied impatiently. After a moment, Meg began singing one of the songs from *Hannibal*. "That's enough." He stopped her after the first few bars.

"Was I that bad?" Meg asked worriedly.

"Of course not, otherwise I wouldn't be bothering to teach you. No, Meg, you are no Carlotta." He smirked up at her. "No, I've heard all I needed to. When I'm ready for you, you'll hear from me. Until then, Mademoiselle, go back to your dancing."

"You have plenty of food, then?" Meg stalled.

"I have everything I need, Meg, except for peace and quiet! Oh, wait. You'll be needing a boat ride, I suppose."

"That won't be necessary. I can swim."

"And freeze your dancing legs off? I think not!" Erik stood and prodded her to the boat. Upon landing at the foot of the stairs, he stopped long enough to let her out, and then he pushed off again. "Remember. You'll hear from me! Until then, keep dancing!" he called back to her. He chuckled as she stormed up the stairs, her torch bouncing in the darkness.

A week passed with no word from her new teacher. Meg's days were filled with an uneasy pattern of practice and preparation for the upcoming production, and she was always glancing around her, looking for some sort of sign from him. She had to tell herself to trust him, that he could take care of himself, and yet her imagination was always running wild, particularly at night. And so, on this night, when she heard his soft voice, she thought for sure that it was a dream. "Angel of Light, come take me away from the darkness. Angel of Light, come quick on the wings of the wind." *Such a lovely dream...* "For goodness sake, Meg, do you not know my voice? Come quickly!" Meg awoke with a start. Yes, it had been Erik hissing just now! She hurriedly crept across the floor to where the back wall was open, but she missed seeing the last bed and stubbed her toe. Before she could cry out, a strong arm pulled her through, the wall closing behind her. His hand quickly came to her mouth, and he dragged her toward the staircase. They were halfway down before he finally allowed her to scream, which she did. Right in his ear. "I beg your pardon. I wasn't expecting Carlotta." She could hear the smirk in his voice.

"Oh, very funny. I suppose it would have been too much trouble for you to warn me about that bed post? And what on earth is the meaning of sending for me at this late hour?"

"My dear girl, if you are to dance in the day, this is the only time you have to sing."

"So I suppose sleep is out of the question."

"You can survive on one less hour every other night." They were at the boat now, and she refused his help in getting in. They were silent on the way to his music cavern, and Meg limped over to the organ. "Now then, that song I was singing is part of a duet I wrote. You have three songs just for yourself, and then the duet. We will begin with that tonight."

"Well, you don't waste any time."

"Silence. Read along while I play." Erik placed a sheet of paper into her hands, and she held it up to the candle light. The song went as follows:

"(Erik): Surrounded by darkness

My senses are everywhere

I hear every movement

And feel every sound in the air

In shadows I've learned to hide

From a world in which I'm despised

Emptiness fills me, Darkness surrounds me

Death cannot be very far away from my side

Angel of Light

Come take me away from the darkness

Angel of Light

Come quick on the wings of the wind

Warm me where I have grown cold

Give new life to where I have grown old

Angel of Light

Angel of Light

(Meg): My name has been called now

By someone who weeps tonight

Cold, broken and weary

A lonely soul needs my light

Candles I'll bring to your side

No longer will you have to hide

Shadows deceive you, But the truth will shine through

When you open your arms wide

Creature of Darkness

Come into my light

Creature of Darkness

Let my warmth and goodness in

Forget all those cold thoughts of fear

Let the shadows of night disappear

Creature of Darkness

Creature of Darkness

(Both) Angel of Light

Come dance with me

Angel of Light

I will choose to be

Out of the Darkness, away from Death's door

When the future calls, I will not fear anymore

I will instead face whatever's in store

For the Angel of Light

Angel of Light

Angel of Light"

"Now, try singing it with me." Erik suggested, and before she could argue, he had begun singing his part. Meg listened to the pain in his voice as he sang the words. "That was your cue, Meg. Pay attention!" He barked, causing her to jump.

"Sorry...I'm ready now." He sang his chorus again, and she started in. As the notes got higher, however, she let her voice fade out.

"I don't believe that was part of the song."

"I...Let me try it again." Erik sighed impatiently, but set her up again. She kept her voice from fading out, but was clearly struggling. "I'm sorry, Erik...It's too high. I can't hit it..."

"Don't you *ever* use that word with me. This is just a run-through, Meg. We'll work on that note next time. For now, just finish it out." The rest of the song went smoothly, and Erik took the music sheet from her and stood up. "Now, Meg, take the boat and get some sleep before you have a bad practice tomorrow. I will see you back here in two nights. Oh, and bring another loaf of bread when you come. I seem to be running out."

"Couldn't I hear the other songs?"

"All in good time. Now go." Erik gently shoved her toward the boat, and she saw him standing on the bank watching her disappear into the darkness. It was all she could do to stay awake long enough to sneak back to her bed, and within minutes, she was sound asleep, the song playing through her dreams.

Chapter Twelve: Erik, The Teacher

"Erik, what are you doing?" Meg stopped singing as soon as Erik began waving his hands around her neck. They were in their third week of lessons, and tonight the hour seemed to drag on longer than usual.

"I'm just looking for the noose that seems to be strangling you."

"Oh, very funny. It's your own fault for writing these notes so high. I tell you, I can't hit them!"

"Meg what have I told you about using that word? Erase 'can't' from your vocabulary this instant!"

"Fine then. It's simply impossible for me to hit those notes." Meg crossed her arms across her chest stubbornly. An exasperated sound escaped Erik's throat as he stood in front of her.

"Look, Meg, don't you think I know what I'm doing?"

"Well, yes, but..."

"And did or did you not place your voice in my care?"

"I..."

"Meg, when I wrote these songs, I wrote them to fit your voice's full potential. Not the way it was, but the way it will be. Did you really think that I would make this easy?"

"No, but I had hoped you would..." Meg admitted.

"Meg, it took ten years for Christine to master her voice and bring it to the level it is now. For you, it might take longer, if you keep arguing and doubting yourself. This will go much smoother if you embrace the possibility of what your voice can be. Now, try it again."

"'When you open your arms wide...'"

"Stop thinking about it so much, Meg. You'll only end up distracting yourself with doubt. Let the music flow naturally. Close your eyes and just sing."

"'Open your arms wide...'" Meg jumped as Erik banged his hands down on the organ keys. "I'm sorry, Erik, I'm really trying..."

"Tell me, Meg, when you begin a new dance routine, how do you go about learning it?"

"I just...listen to the music and move with it..."

"Exactly. You don't think about memorizing steps, do you?"

"Well, no, but singing is an entirely different thing. I'm not as gifted in that area."

"There's that self-doubt again! I'll not have it in these caverns, do you hear me?"

"Yes..." Meg hung her head.

"Let's move down to the last chorus, where we sing together. I want you to listen to my voice and then use it to support your own voice."

"But I'm not supposed to think about it..."

"Oh, just sing!" Erik began singing, and Meg hurried to join his voice. Their voices smoothly played off of each other, and the ending came all too quickly. "Just as I thought. You're used to singing in a group, blending and harmonizing, aren't you?"

"Of course...I am a chorus girl after all."

" Perhaps it is time for you to work on the first of your solo pieces. We'll return to the duet once you've mastered this song." Erik shuffled through some pages until he pulled out a single sheet of paper entitled 'Music Box Dancer'. As he played, Meg read through the words.

"I am a little dancing girl

Bolted down to this tiny stage

Wind me up and I'll dance for you

For as long as the music plays

Day after day or night after night

How I long to escape this plight

Is there no one to dance with me?

Am I destined to never be free

To dance on my own

No one to stop me

From twirling and spinning

Leaping and twisting

Dancing as long as I can

All too soon the music slows

And I am back to face the night alone

As a simple little music box dancing girl."

"We'll begin work on that next time. Right now we're out of time."

"May I just say that this song sounds absolutely beautiful?"

"It will be more so when you add your voice to it, Meg. Now go." Erik smiled.

"Meg, where have you been?" Madame Giry met her daughter in the hallway just outside of the dorm room.

"I, uh...was getting a drink..." Meg chewed her lower lip.

"For one full hour? Don't lie to me, Meg."

"Oh, Mama, it was supposed to be a surprise...I've been taking singing lessons."

"Singing lessons? From Erik?"

"Yes, Mama, from Erik." Meg watched as a cloud of horror came over Madame Giry's face. "Mama, is something wrong?" she asked worriedly.

"Yes, Meg, something is wrong, and I'm going to put a stop to it right now! You will take me to him immediately."

"Oh, but I'm tired, Mama..."

"That is your own fault, my dear. Now come." Meg reluctantly led Madame Giry down to the boat, and they slowly made their way to where he was hunched over the organ, furiously writing.

"Back so soon, Meg? I would think you would want to give your voice a rest."

"Erik, we need to talk." Madame Giry spoke up, and Erik jumped before whirling around on the bench.

"Ah, Antoinette. To what do I owe this pleasant surprise of a visit?"

"There is nothing pleasant about it, Erik. What is the meaning of dragging my daughter away from her much needed sleep?"

"Madame Giry, I am well aware of Meg's commitment to her dancing, and I have only required one hour every other night for the past three weeks. Are you saying that her dancing has been lacking?"

"Not exceptionally, no. But what am I supposed to think when I see her sneaking off for an hour in the night, hmm? Tell me that!"

"Yes, your concern is understandable. Forgive me for leaving you out of my plans from the beginning."

"Perhaps if we change the lessons to once or twice a month?" Meg spoke up.

"*Once* a month sounds reasonable." Madame Giry nodded.

"I will agree only on the condition that Meg takes her songs and practices them once a week." Erik replied.

"Yes, I can live with that," Meg smiled, and Erik turned and handed her the two songs he had played for her.

"Very well. I will expect you on the third Monday of every month. As for your usual gift of bread and vegetables, I will expect a full month's supply when you come for your lessons. Agreed?"

"Agreed. Good night, Monsieur." Meg curtsied and returned to the boat.

"Erik, I warn you. Many years ago, you made a promise to me. I expect you to uphold that promise."

"Antoinette, I assure you that harming your daughter is furthest from my mind."

"See that it stays there." Madame Giry gave him one last warning look before joining her daughter at the boat. Silently, Erik watched as the boat disappeared across the lake.

By the end of summer, Meg had mastered 'Music Box Dancer' and another song Erik had shown her, 'Shadow Ballet'. Meg had to hand it to him for sticking to a subject close to her heart in each of the songs, and she told him so, to which he replied, "Mademoiselle, I have seen you dance, and I must say that your talent is an inspiration in itself." With each new song, the notes gradually became higher up in Meg's vocal range, and Erik was pleased to see that it seemed to be working to raise her confidence level. Madame Giry couldn't help noticing that Meg's new confidence carried into her dancing, and she was soon becoming very popular with the opera goers. Erik stuck to his promise to Carlotta, however, and restrained himself from 'helping' Meg to be cast as the leads. It was the managers who began casting Meg in larger roles, and Meg accepted them graciously. After a short while, however, she found herself missing dancing in the background, and so, when the next production was announced, Meg privately begged her mother to keep the managers from casting her in anything outside of the chorus girls and regular dancers.

This move on her part did not go unnoticed, however, and when she went down for her next lesson, Erik was waiting for her amongst a mess of overturned music stands and scattered sheet music. "Tell me, Meg, are you ashamed of my teaching you?"

"Of course not, Monsieur..."

"Skip the formalities, Meg, for once! You might as well have slapped me in the face, do you know that?" The fury in his voice was so strong that Meg took a step back, her heel on the verge of slipping out from under her. She reminded herself that she was still dangerously close to the edge of the lake.

"Erik, I wasn't trying to..."

"Don't you dare speak to me! I know for a fact that you refused a secondary role. If you've lost interest in singing, please tell me so that I may stop wasting my time teaching you!"

"It's not that...I'm just more comfortable in the background, that's all..."

"Comfort? *Comfort?* My dear pupil, you gave that privilege up when you first came down here and found me. You knew that by asking me to teach you, you would forgo the luxury of comfort once again!"

"Erik, stop and just listen to me! You said yourself that you wanted me to keep my dancing as my top priority. That is exactly what I'm doing! I know how passionate you are about your music, but don't let it cloud your judgment. You should know by now how much trouble that can get you into!"

"Get out of my sight! Lessons are canceled this month, seeing as it seems that's what you want. I don't want to see you down here until you have learned to fully embrace what I have to teach you." Erik turned away from her then, and he refused to look in her direction until the boat had disappeared.

Chapter Thirteen: Confrontation

Meg threw herself onto the bed, her sobs shaking her whole body. *How in the world did Christine survive those lessons?* Of course, Erik had taught her from behind walls and masks, which created an almost dreamlike atmosphere to her lessons. And of course, Erik would have been gentler with Christine, seeing as she was the object of his affection. Meg sighed. Perhaps he was right. Perhaps she was throwing all his hard work back in his face. *No...the limelight is just not for me! The sooner he understands that, the better. I know I'm right, and he's just going to have to live with *that!* Finally, Meg fell asleep, a determined smile on her face.

The next night, Meg crept down to the cellars, making sure to guide the boat silently through the waters. Before she rounded the corner, however, she heard his voice, singing in all its sweetness and sadness. Her heart fell...it was their duet, and he was finishing his part. Taking a deep breath, she joined in, quietly at first, but as she neared that one troublesome line, something in her broke free, and the notes rang smoothly throughout the caverns. He brought his head up from his hands then, and watched as she brought the boat to it's landing spot. She grinned widely as she continued with her chorus. "' Creature of Darkness, come into my light. Creature of Darkness Let my warmth and goodness in...'" Slowly, teacher and pupil approached each other, and when she finished, he joined her for the last chorus. During the final line, Erik pulled her into an embrace, which she warmly returned.

"Welcome back, Mademoiselle. I see you are ready to continue your lessons."

"Erik, before we begin, we need to reach an understanding. I came down here, fully prepared to make you see my point of view, no matter how long it took. But singing just now...I don't know what happened. Something inside me just...broke free..."

"What is it you wanted to tell me?"

"Promise you'll remain calm?"

"I promise." Erik sat down on his organ bench, and Meg took a seat in one of the wooden chairs across from him.

"Erik, as wonderful a teacher as you are, and as beautiful as these songs may be, I cannot put my dancing on a back burner while I pursue improving my voice. Perhaps on special occasions, I would gladly perform as a singer, but for the regular productions, I would be much happier to step back and dance with the others. The limelight may suit Carlotta and Christine well, but it's just not for me. Am I making sense?"

"As much as I hate to admit it, yes, you are making sense. I would be lying if I said I wasn't disappointed, however."

"I know how much you've put into teaching me, Erik, and I really do appreciate all that you've done for me. It's not like I'm saying that I don't wish to continue learning from you." Meg reached her hand toward him, and when he took it, something clicked inside the both of them. Slowly, he pulled her to him, into another embrace. Just as suddenly, however, he pulled away, walking down to the lake. Tears began to flow. *No...I can't let it happen. Not again.* "Erik?"

"Go back to bed now, Meg. I'll see you in a month." He refused to look at her, and instead of watching her leave, he slowly made his way to his bed, weeping quietly into the pillow.

As the autumn months came and went, Meg's lessons continued and her voice gradually improved. However, something had obviously changed, and she soon found that the lesson times were being reduced to a half hour. Erik seemed to distance himself more and more, sometimes by yelling at her tiniest mistakes, other times by simply walking away from her. She found it harder and harder to leave him, knowing that it would be a month before she would see him again. She could not dwell on her sadness, however, so she threw herself into the various dance routines.

Mid-November, it was announced that the managers would be staging a private show for their most loyal audience members which would take place the weekend before Christmas. Each performer would be given the opportunity to put something together for it, either as a solo or a group. To add to Meg's delight, Madame Giry told her that Raoul and Christine would be in the city at that time, and would most definitely be seeing the performance. "Will you be singing or dancing, Meg?" Madame Giry questioned.

"I owe it to Erik to choose singing, Mama. In fact, I know just the piece, if I can just convince him..."

"Convince him?" Madame Giry cast her a sidelong glance.

"Oh, you'll see, Mama. I need to talk with him first, and if he agrees, I'll let you be the first to know." While everyone else was focused on making up their minds, Meg skipped down the hallway. She took a detour at the kitchen to grab one of the fresh-baked pastries, and then quickly made her way down to where her teacher was. As he came into view, she silently giggled at his confused face. Bringing the boat to a stop, she jumped out and waved the pastry in front of him. "Oh, Erik...I have a favor to ask of you..."

"And I suppose agreeing to it would earn me a bite of that pastry?" Erik feigned disinterest, but his mouth watered at the sight of the pastry covered in icing, and he could see a bit of chocolate filling oozing out of one of the sides. *How long has it been since I've tasted something sweet? A lifetime, it seems...*

"You catch on quickly. It seems that we will be putting on a special performance just before Christmas, and we are all getting the opportunity to perform on our own or as a group. I was thinking about singing."

"That's an excellent choice, Mademoiselle." Erik slowly reached for the pastry, but she slapped his hand away.

"I was thinking about singing our duet." Erik met her gaze then, and the realization hit.

"You want me to sing with you?"

"That's exactly what I'm asking."

"Why can't you choose something else? You sing 'Music Box Dancer' rather beautifully."

"'Angel of Light' is even prettier. Besides, if I choose something else, you won't be getting this pastry." Meg smirked.

"Meg, even if I do agree, I doubt that the managers would welcome the idea of me performing on that stage again. Remember what happened last time?"

"I'm sure my mother will help us convince them that nothing like that will happen again. Please, Erik? For me?" *There were those eyes again...* Erik sighed.

"Alright, Meg. I suppose there won't be any peace around here unless I agree. You may tell the managers that I will be joining you. But don't be surprised if they say no."

"Thank you, Erik." Meg smiled and handed over the pastry, which he gobbled up in just a few bites. Meg giggled at the ring of chocolate and pastry crumbs that appeared around his mouth and on the tip of his nose, and she dampened a cloth to wipe it away.

It took some convincing, but the night of the performance showcase, Erik stood backstage with Meg, waiting for their turn to perform. He had borrowed another costume from the prop department, and now he stood dressed all in black, complete with a black mask similar to the *Don Juan*one. Meg, on the other hand, was in her masquerade angel costume, without the mask. They stood somewhat apart from the other performers, as they could sense the uneasiness around the man formerly known as 'Opera Ghost'. Finally, Alyce and the rest of her group of young dancers made their way offstage, and Erik took a deep breath. Monsieur Andre announced their song, and Meg had to gently drag him into the spotlight. Erik stared at the audience nervously, but as soon as the music started, he flew through his part with confidence. Meg sang her verses perfectly, and as they joined their voices, Erik sensed the beauty of the moment, and he took both of Meg's hands as they reached the middle of the chorus. They gazed into each others eyes, and the rest of the room faded away. All too soon, the last note was sung, and the applause pulled them back into reality. They took a bow and made their way offstage, where Carlotta was eagerly awaiting her second number. "Meg, that was beautiful!" Alyce whispered.

"That was Erik's doing entirely. He wrote that song." Meg grinned.

"You are very talented, Monsieur." Alyce curtsied.

"Thank you. Meg was the inspiration for that piece, however."

One person was not pleased with the performance, however, and before the two singers could join the rest of the cast for the celebration, Madame Giry pulled them into the hallway outside her quarters. "Erik, I'm not going to beat around the bush. I want you to stop teaching Meg."

"Mama, what are you talking about? I'm not letting my dancing suffer..."

"This has nothing to do with your dancing, Marguerite. It has everything to do with me not wanting to see you get hurt."

"But I'm not hurting, Mama..."

"Silence! I saw the look in your eyes, the both of you! And I will not, *will not* allow you to become his next Christine."

"How dare you, Antoinette! I have no intention of using your daughter as a replacement, and I'm surprised that you think so low of me!"

"It does not matter if you intend it or not. I know what I saw tonight, and I will not allow it to continue. I want you to stay away from my daughter, Erik. I'll not just stand by and watch you break her heart."

"Mama, I don't understand. The only way my heart would be broken is if I was forced to never see Erik again!" Meg burst into tears of confusion. "He's my friend, Mama, my friend and my teacher."

"There was far more than friendship in your eyes tonight, Marguerite. You will do as I say. Now leave us." Sobbing, Meg quickly hugged Erik before making her way to her dorm room. As soon as the door was closed, Erik turned to face Antoinette, anger in his face.

"Now, Antoinette, suppose you explain to me why you would do this to your daughter."

"Erik, you and Meg could turn blue in the face denying it, but I know what I saw. You love each other."

"Antoinette, I..."

"There, you see? Denying it already! You may not see it now, but I certainly do. And it will never work. I refuse to allow Meg to spend the rest of her life down in your caverns."

"Then I will simply purchase a house here in the city." Erik reasoned, but then he saw a new look in her face. "You don't think I belong in the surface world, do you?"

"I did not say that, Erik."

"No, but your face certainly did. Admit it, Madame Giry. You think I deserve to spend the rest of my days alone."

"Erik, you have spent your whole life apart from society. You would never survive out there away from the opera house. This is your home. This is where you belong."

"Honestly, Antoinette, I expected better of you. I can picture anyone saying those words to me, anyone except you. I see now that our friendship was as real as 'the Phantom'."

"I am sorry you see it that way, Erik. I'm only trying to protect you and Meg. That is all." Madame Giry grasped Erik's arm, forcing him to listen as she sang "Learn to Be Lonely."

Before Erik could respond, Madame Giry moved past him to join in the festivities. Erik slid to the floor, sobbing into his arms while the ache in his heart grew more and more painful. *What is the point of gaining back my heart only to have it shattered all over again?*

Chapter Fourteen: Christmas Break

Christmas morning was soon upon them all, and long before the break of dawn, Meg slipped out of her bed, retrieving a wrapped parcel from under the mattress. Slowly, she crept into the kitchen to gather a few extra items, and then made her way silently down into the caverns. He had taken the boat, of course, but Meg didn't even think of that. She absentmindedly waded through the freezing lake water until she saw him. He was sitting at the organ, his back to her, and he was just staring at the keys as if in a trance. "Merry Christmas, Erik..." Her soft voice echoed off the walls of the cavern, and he slowly turned to face her.

"Meg, you should not be here."

"I'll not stay long. I have but two hours before Mama will be looking for me. I just wanted to give you this. It's not much, and I'm far from being a talented artist, but I want you to have it anyway. As a gift and as a thank you for being such a wonderful teacher." Meg handed him the package, and he let it sit in his lap for the longest time. "You have to open it, silly," Meg managed a smile, and he slowly undid the ribbons and paper. Finally, he held up the gift. Meg had found a discarded half-face mask from the prop room, and she had used flesh-colored paint and makeup to cover it, making it appear far more natural. "I know you said that masks are in your past, but I just figured, if you ever decide to leave here, this might help..."

"Thank you, Meg. I, too, have a gift for you." Erik shuffled over to his bed and took a small unwrapped object out from under one of the pillows. As he brought it closer, she squealed in delight.

"Ballet slippers! Did you make these?"

"Where else would I have gotten them?"

"Oh, Erik, they're beautiful!" Quickly she slid them onto her feet and did a small dance routine.

"I had to guess at the size."

"Oh, they fit perfectly! And you even put beads on them!" Meg gave him a big hug then, and slowly he brought his arms up to return it.

"I...see you brought more food. I still have plenty." He pulled away, motioning to the basket.

"Well, after all, it's Christmas, and you deserve a special dinner just as much as the rest of us."

"Would you care to join me for a small breakfast, then, Meg?" *What are you doing? Madame Giry will have your hide for sure!*

"I would love to, but we should make it quick." Meg brought the basket over to the bed and began setting out some of the sweet rolls onto cloth napkins, and they sat across from one another, eating in silence. Neither dared to speak, for they knew that all too soon, they would have to part again, possibly for good. Yes, even as we speak, the tiny meal was done, and a single tear made its way down Meg's cheek.

"Don't waste your tears on me, Meg. Your mother is right in that you deserve far more than I could ever give you."

"Now who's the one with self-doubt?" Meg forced a half-smile, but she felt her lower lip tremble, and she turned away.

"Meg, I speak the truth. You have your whole life ahead of you. You should spend it on the stage, dazzling audiences for years to come. Soon, you'll have a whole line of suitors to choose from, and I'm sure your mother will make sure that none of them turn out to be Fredriques. You'll marry and have a happy, full life, and somewhere in there, you'll forget about me."

"Erik, I could never forget you! You've given me so much...you mean so much to me..." Meg choked out through her sobs, and Erik pulled her to him so she could cry into his chest. *Oh, how I'll miss this feeling of holding you in my arms...*

"Come. I'll take you back in the boat."

"Will you walk me to the mirror, one last time?" Meg gulped.

"One last time, Meg. And when you step into that room, do not look back. You must be brave."

"I'll try, Erik." Meg wiped her hand across her tear-streaked face, and Erik placed a gentle kiss on her forehead. The journey back was silent, and when they reached the mirror, Meg allowed her hand to linger in his a few minutes longer, until he finally pulled his hand away, escaping into the darkness before she could see the tears running down his face.

Antoinette watched as Meg shuffled into the dorm room, barely mumbling a 'good night'. For a single moment, the ballet instructor questioned as to whether or not she had done the right thing. To see her daughter so sad on Christmas of all days, knowing she had been the cause of it, was almost too much to bear. But no, she knew she was right. Her daughter would see in time that this was for the best. Perhaps Madame Giry hadn't been able to stop Erik from going after Christine, but at least she had seen that look in his eyes in time to stop him from pursuing Meg and destroying everything in the process. Yes, Meg would see in time. Until then, Antoinette would make herself much more approachable than she had been.

After making a quick trip to the kitchen, Antoinette carried a steaming cup of chocolate into the dorm room. Most of the other girls were still celebrating, either with the other performers or with their own families at home, and it was still early enough that Meg was alone. As Antoinette entered the room, she found her daughter laying on her side, her body shaking as she sobbed. Antoinette sat down on the bed, rubbing the dancer's shoulder. "Oh, Meg, my daughter...I know it hurts now, but the pain won't last long."

"How can you say that? The longer I'm away from him, the more it hurts!"

"Come, sit up. Here, I brought you some chocolate."

"I don't want it."

"But you hardly had a bite to eat all day."

"I'm not hungry."

"Somehow I don't believe that, Marguerite. Christine tells me you barely spoke a word to her. She's very worried about you."

"Did you tell her my reason?"

"I thought I might leave that up to you. She and Raoul have invited you to stay with them in the country for a couple of weeks."

"I suppose you accepted for me."

"Of course. You two are like sisters, and I think you deserve a change of scenery for a while. They will be leaving tomorrow afternoon, and you will be going with them." Antoinette stood up and set the chocolate on the floor beside Meg's bed before placing a kiss on her cheek. "Good night, Meg. I hope you know that I do love you." There was no response from her daughter, and Antoinette left the room. She was pleased the next morning, however, when she found that the mug was empty.

    For two days straight, Erik did nothing but pace the cavern floor, stopping only to eat, and even then it was only a nibble or two. He kept his mind completely blank, knowing that if he dared to allow the tiniest thought to go through his mind, it would throw him back into the state in which Meg had found him. At first, he had tried to be strong, for Meg's sake. He had even gone so far as to agree with Antoinette a little bit, that the separation was for the best, and that perhaps Meg had gotten too close. But then he had remembered all the little things. He remembered Meg's gentle touch on his face when he was still too weak to sit up. He remembered how her head had felt buried into his chest and how it didn't take much to change her frown into an adorable giggle. He recalled what it had felt like to watch Meg being attacked, and how enraged he had been to see her so helpless. He thought of all those singing lessons and how frustrating it was for him to see clearly where he could take her voice when she couldn't see it herself. And then, he forced himself to remember the night of their performance. He remembered looking deep into her eyes, knowing that she was doing the same thing. He had seen it then, even if he wasn't ready to admit it. And he knew right then and there that he loved Marguerite Giry, in all her stubbornness and innocence. *But what's the use of loving her now? She's gone! She does not belong in my darkness! She belongs to the world!* By the time his fit of rage was over, three candelabras and two chairs had joined all his masks and wigs in the bottom of the lake, and he sat on the floor, not even bothering to wipe the tears away.

    Several hours passed before he was finally able to stand up. A spark of his old determination returned, and it was all he needed. He knew Meg cared deeply for him, at least as a close friend, and he vowed right then and there that he wasn't going to let her disappear from his life. As long as she was away, he knew his heart would remain shattered. He did not know what would happen once he had her back in his arms, but he knew that if they stood together, they would be able to face whatever life threw at them.

With this thought in mind, he finally made his way up to the dorm room. Peeking in, however, he saw that it was empty. *Of course. She's probably out dancing somewhere, erasing me from her mind.* Cautiously, he slipped through the secret doorway, and he had just reached her bed when he saw Madame Giry pass by in the direction of her quarters. He hesitated for only a moment. *Oh no. I won't back down. Not this time.* Swiftly, he entered the corridor and was able to corner Antoinette before she could open her door. "Erik, what are you doing here?"

"Where is she?"

"Now, Erik, I thought I had made myself clear..."

"Oh, you made yourself clear as glass, Antoinette. Now allow me to make myself even clearer. I have always had nothing but respect for you, but your most recent words aimed at me served only to all but sever that respect. You of all people should know that when two people love each other, anything that stands between them is quickly defeated."

"Erik, this is exactly why I did what I did. You are acting on feelings alone! For once, will you use that genius brain of yours and think? What kind of mother would I be if I allow my daughter to go into a future as uncertain as yours? What happens if you do go out into the world and you find it as unkind as you left it? What then? Am I to just sit back and watch my daughter be forced to go into hiding?"

"Madame Giry, I tried to see things from that point of view. I spent a whole day trying to make myself believe that what you say is true. All it did was to show me how much I love your daughter. Whether or not you agree with me is entirely your choice. But there is nothing you can do to make me stop loving her. Now, where is Meg?" He locked eyes with her, and allowed the icy daggers to fly through his stare and through his voice. Finally, Antoinette dropped her gaze.

"She is visiting Christine in the country."

"For how long?"

"Two weeks. It was Christine's idea. They have not spent very much time together this past year."

"And Meg went willingly?"

"She did not fight, if that's what you're asking." He could sense that she was holding back, but he didn't need to hear it. Her eyes said it all.

"You accepted for her, didn't you? You wanted to get her away from me, did you not?"

"Please, Erik, it is not for a lifetime. She will be back."

"No, I cannot wait that long. How far from the city does Christine live?"

"A day's journey at least, and that is by carriage."

"Was there any money left after the reconstruction?"

"Yes, plenty."

"Good. You will withdraw my remaining funds immediately and arrange a carriage to take me to her in the morning. I will meet you in this spot no later than dawn."

"And if I refuse?"

"Madame, our friendship is hanging by a single thread this very moment. Now is not the time to be testing that thread's strength." He made sure that she heard the threatening tone to his voice before he turned to go back to his caverns. He had some planning to do.

Chapter Fifteen: Choices

"Meg, you've been stirring your tea for twenty minutes now. What is it?" Christine placed her hand on Meg's, forcing her to drop the spoon with a sigh.

"I know exactly what you're going to say, so there's no point in me telling you."

"Come on, Meg, that's not fair. The point would be to stop me from worrying."

"I didn't ask you to worry about me."

"Meg, it's me, remember? We tell each other everything. And we've shared so much...remember when we poured green paint into Carlotta's perfume bottle?" Christine giggled at the memory, and Meg allowed a smile to spread across her face.

"I think all of Europe heard her screams!" she recalled.

"Your mother wouldn't let us out of her sight for a month!" Christine pointed, and Meg let her smile fade. "Oh, Meg, you've got to tell me what's bothering you! What has happened to my warm, lively friend, hmm?"

"Really, I mustn't tell you. It hurts too much just thinking about it..." Meg stood and crossed the dining room to stare out the window. The de Chagny estate really was beautiful, set on the river bank with snow-covered fields and trees as far as the eye could see. But all Meg saw were prison bars across the window and an endless gray sky.

"You're in love, aren't you?" Christine was standing behind her now, and Meg whirled around, surprise on her face.

"How did you know?"

"Oh, Meg, I know that very feeling! It's really nothing to be ashamed of! Now tell me, who is it?"

"Now *that* I'll definitely not be telling you." Meg turned away.

"Oh, but..." Just then, Raoul entered the room, and Meg breathed a silent sigh of relief.

"Sorry to interrupt, but it appears that a carriage just pulled through the gates. Were you expecting anyone?"

"No...were you?"

"If I was, I would not have asked. It must be urgent." With that, the three of them made their way into the foyer, where the butler was just opening the front door.

"Erik!" Meg rushed forward, leaping into his arms before he had a chance to step fully into the mansion.

"Meg...this...is...who...?" Christine stuttered, suddenly feeling faint.

"I assume, then, that you know this man?" The butler questioned.

"Yes...he's...an old friend from Paris. Thank you, Jacques." Raoul dismissed the butler. "Please, Erik, do come in." Raoul led the way into the parlor, and while he and Christine took two of the chairs, Erik and Meg chose the sofa.

"I don't intend on staying very long. I just came to fetch Meg." Erik cleared his throat.

"Why? Did something happen at the opera house? Did the Madame fall ill?"

"No, nothing like that. Everything is fine."

"It appears, Raoul, that our two visitors have fallen in love." Christine spoke carefully, as if trying to convince herself of it. As the truth finally made its way out into the open, Erik and Meg looked at each other, finally smiling.

"And how does the Madame feel about this?" Raoul's tone was both guarded and protective.

"What she feels does not change how I feel." Erik spoke bluntly.

"I'm sorry, Erik, but while Meg is here, we must honor her mother's wishes."

"Did I not say that I am here to *fetch* Meg? Say the word, and we will be gone."

"On the contrary. *You* will be gone. Meg is to remain here for the duration her mother and my wife agreed upon."

"Christine, say something! You said yourself that you see the love between Erik and myself." Meg whispered.

"I'm sorry, Meg, but Raoul is my husband. I must honor his decision and side with him."

"Dinner is served," Jacques announced before the conversation could grow any more heated.

"Erik, you are welcome to join us and stay the night, as I'm sure your journey was long and tiring. I expect you and you alone to be on your way following breakfast." Raoul stood. Erik remained silent, however, for the remainder of the evening.

That night, he walked Meg to her door, Christine and Raoul not far behind. Under their watchful eyes, he could not do what he wished and pull Meg into a never-ending embrace, and so he simply brushed a lock of her golden hair out of her face before bidding her a simple 'good night.' He hoped, however, that as she looked into his eyes, she would see the love pouring out of his gaze. She looked up at him, a half-smile on her face that told him that she knew. That was all he needed. He nodded then, and moved on down the corridor to one of the other guest chambers.

Behind closed doors, the Vicomte and Vicomtess spoke in whispered voices in regards to their guests as they prepared for bed. "Raoul, are you sure that we are doing the right thing?" Christine began, brushing her long, dark curls.

"Christine, Meg is a guest in our home, which puts her under my protection. I cannot in good conscience betray that responsibility."

"Yes, I know that, Raoul, and I don't expect you to. I just hate seeing Meg so sad." As Christine set her brush down on the vanity, her husband came up behind her and wrapped his arms around her, kissing the top of her head.

"Your caring attitude is one of the many things I love you for, Little Lottie. But we cannot allow it to come before doing what is right."

"I just wish I knew how to cheer Meg up in the meantime." Christine sighed. Raoul gently lifted her to her feet and turned her around, covering her lips with his.

"We have tomorrow to think about that. Tonight, we have each other." He pulled her to their bed then, and soon they were covering each other in passionate kisses long into the night.

"Meg...Meg, wake up..." A whispered voice called. Meg sighed and opened her eyes. After all, she hadn't really been asleep. She quickly lit one of the bedside lamps and turned to face the balcony, where the voice had come from. On the other side of the glass doors, she could see Erik looking in at her, ignoring the chill of the early January night.

"Erik, for goodness sake..." Meg hurried to open the doors and pulled him into the warmth. "Are you mad? What would they think if they saw you?" She threw the top blanket over his shoulders as he grasped her hands.

"Forgive me, Meg, but I needed a chance to speak with you alone. What was said today...I need to know that our feelings are mutual before I go any further with my plans. If you do not share my feelings, I will quietly slip away, as Raoul wishes, and will not bother you anymore."

"Erik, of course I love you! When I first saw you lying there in all your sorrow, I took pity on you. As I watched you struggle with your fears and heal from your sickness, I knew that I cared about you. After my attack, when I stopped you from leaving, I knew we could be friends. I found myself looking up to you when you tended to my arm, when you rescued me, and when you persisted with teaching me. But now, standing here, I know that what we have is more than a friendship. I don't know when or where it happened, Erik, but I love you with all that is within me, and if we ever part again, my life will surely be over."

"There you go, being dramatic again," Erik smirked.

"Oh, but what are we to do with this love?" Meg sighed.

"I do have a plan, Meg, but it would require you do something that I know you aren't ready to do."

"Erik, whatever it is, I'll do it." A look of determination filled her face.

"I would not say that before hearing it, Meg. I simply cannot bring myself to ask it of you."

"Please, Erik, what is it?" She wrapped her arms around him, and he placed his arm around her shoulders.

"We would have to leave tonight. You would have to leave behind all you have ever known and loved. We would be on our own, making our own decisions, without Christine and Raoul, and without your mother." At those words, Meg slowly pulled away and sat down on her bed.

"Tonight?"

"The only other option is to honor your mother's wishes. You would return to the opera house and keep dancing. I would leave for some time, until I find us a place to live and a way to earn a living. It could take months or even years."

"Oh, Erik, I could never bear to be away from you that long." A tear trickled down Meg's cheek as she turned to face him.

"But can you bear to deny your mother and your best friend? Are you prepared to live on the run?"

"Oh, Erik, I don't know! I just don't know! When did the world become suddenly so very complicated?"

"My dear Marguerite, the world has always been complicated. You just haven't been outside the walls of the opera house long enough to see that until now. There comes a time when one is forced to suddenly grow up without being fully ready for it. That time for me came at a much younger age than you are now. I wish there was some way for me to make this easier for you or help you make up your mind, but the choice is entirely up to you." Erik sat down on the bed next to her, pulling her head to his chest. He held her sobbing, shaking body for several minutes before she finally lifted her head with a sigh.

"Erik, the future is under a heavy fog of uncertainty, no matter what I decide. Not you or I or Mama or Christine or Raoul could possibly know what might happen tomorrow or a year from now. All I know is what I feel when I'm with you, and how much it hurts to be away from you. Everyone I know and love has turned their backs on us, but maybe one day they'll see that this is right. Erik, I choose to stay by your side no matter what. I choose you." Slowly, Meg brought her face closer to his, and their lips met. The kiss was soft and careful at first, but it soon grew more passionate. Finally, as Erik realized how little time they had, he reluctantly pulled away.

"You'd best pack your things, but pack light. We'll leave a note if you'd like, but then we must be off."

"Yes, a note would be a good idea. I do not want them to worry any more than they have to." Meg quickly threw a couple dresses into her satchel, along with her new ballet slippers and her hairbrush. "Erik, turn away so that I may change. I'll not wander through the snow in my nightgown." Erik was quick to obey, and Meg quickly dressed in her warmest clothes. She found a sheet of blank paper and quickly scrawled out a note, telling her friends not to worry and promising to keep in touch as often as possible. Erik added his own promise to put Meg's safety and welfare before his own no matter what, and they placed the note on Meg's pillow.

"Are you ready, Meg?"

"As ready as I'll ever be..." Meg wrapped her cloak around her shoulders and followed him onto the balcony. Erik picked up his own satchel and led the way down the rope and onto the snowy ground. Silently, they fled across the field and into the unknown.

Chapter Sixteen: A Surprise Reunion

By the time their absence was discovered, Erik had found a small grove of trees in which they could rest for the day. It was small enough to not pose a threat, yet thick enough so that they would remain well hidden. Meg shivered as she huddled close to him, and he wrapped his own cape around the both of them. "Sleep now, Meg. We'll continue on just before dusk."

"Do you have any idea as to where we're going?"

"Before I left Paris, I was able to study a map of this area. It appears that there is a small village nearby. If we travel by night, we should reach it by the end of the week." He watched as Meg started to say something in reply, but it came out as a yawn as she rested her head on his shoulder. Erik remained awake for a few hours more, watching the sky. They had regrettably left a clear trail of footprints, but he also noticed that dark clouds were forming. Snow would come shortly and hopefully erase their path. Satisfied that they were out of danger, he pulled his cape even tighter around them and joined Meg in sleep.

As dusk fell, Erik was immediately aware of the pile of snow covering them. He gently used the inside of his cape to brush the snow out of Meg's hair, causing her to wake up with a shiver. "Are you ready to keep moving?"

"I think so...where are the bags?" Meg slowly got to her feet.

"It snowed today." Erik bent down and uncovered the satchels before reaching into his. He pulled out a bit of bread and divided it. "I know it's not much, but it will keep us from starving."

"It's plenty, Erik." Meg smiled at him reassuringly. They walked slowly at first, allowing the tiny meal to last. By the time they had finished, they had come to a well-traveled road, and they decided that their footprints would be less noticeable there.

The next two nights of traveling were fairly uneventful, and they always managed to find some trees or large rocks to hide behind during the day. At one point, just before the break of dawn, they reached the top of a hill, and Erik could make out the faint outline of the village off in the distance. Before he could say anything, however, the wind suddenly picked up as snow began falling heavily. "Meg, we're going to have to keep going until we reach the village. Can you make it?"

"I...think so..." Meg pulled her cloak tighter around herself, and Erik could see in her face how weak she had become.

"Here...give me your bag..." He placed his own satchel under one arm and grasped hers with the same hand. Wrapping his free arm around her, he pulled her along with him in the direction of the village. In a matter of seconds, all he could see in front of him was the blanket of falling snow, and he closed his eyes to protect them from the icy wind. He could not count how many times they stumbled in the deep snow, nor did he remember each time he picked them both up. All he could think about was when Meg collapsed beside him, too cold to shiver and too weak to pull herself up. Blindly, Erik dropped the bags and removed his cape. Wrapping it completely around Meg, he then placed the satchels on her before lifting her into his arms. He had but taken ten steps before stumbling again, and this time tears held him to the ground. He could only manage to use his own body to shelter her from the cold before completely surrendering to his thoughts and fears. "I'm sorry, Meg, I tried...I failed you...I failed your mother...I'm so sorry my love..."

"Was that a knock at the door?" The elderly widow asked from her bed.

"It more than likely was the wind. It seems a blizzard has started." Her son-in-law replied in a dismissive tone from the breakfast table.

"No, Jean-Claude, I heard it too...and now it sounds like someone crying..." His wife stepped away from the stove to peer out the cottage window. At first, all she saw was white, but as she narrowed her gaze in on the doorstep, she could make out a dark figure huddled against the dimness of dawn. "Yes, there is someone there!" She exclaimed, and her husband was quick to open the wooden door. The sobbing man barely acknowledged the warmth of their home, and they noticed a young woman in his arms.

"Monsieur, come inside quickly!" Jean-Claude's voice was urgent, and the unexpected visitor slowly rose to his feet. Before he looked at them, he knelt down to lift his companion. Once inside, he set her down on the one sofa, brushing the frozen locks of hair out of her face.

"Is she ill?" Marie questioned.

"Only from cold and hunger. I thank you for the shelter, and we will not trouble you long."

"Nonsense. You will stay as long as you need. Come, I was just about to serve breakfast." Erik was hesitant to leave Meg's side, but the fragrant aroma coming from the kitchen finally got his feet moving to follow.

"Claire! Come down to breakfast now!" Marie called up to the loft. Slowly a little girl of about five or six appeared at the top of the ladder.

"Coming, Mama!" As she made her way down the ladder, Erik noticed a worn-out rag doll clutched in her arms. Reaching the lower floor, the girl turned around and immediately noticed Erik. "Mama, who's that?"

"My name's Erik, and the girl on the sofa is Meg." Even if Erik hadn't been too cold and weak to think up false names, he saw no point in deceiving those helping them. Especially not this little girl who looked at him not with fear, but with complete curiosity and innocence that matched Meg's personality.

"Erik..." The widow had risen from her bed to investigate the excitement at the door, and as she repeated his name in a whispered voice, she immediately felt faint.

"Mama, you should not be up!" Marie rushed to her mother's side.

"Forgive me daughter, but...bring me closer...I need to be sure..." Ever so slowly, Marie brought the widow closer to Erik, and the elderly woman gasped.

"You look as though you've seen a ghost, Mama..." Jean-Claude remarked.

"I apologize, Madame...if my face bothers you, I have a mask in my bag..." Erik turned his face away.

"No...no, a mask will not erase the face I have held in my heart all these years..." The widow brought her hand to his face, caressing the scars. "All my life, I never imagined living to see you again, Erik. When I gave you up, I felt that I had given up all rights to even dreaming of it. But here you are...here you are, my son."

Erik stared into the woman's eyes, then, and immediately his very first memory surfaced in his mind. Those eyes that had been so full of tears had stared into his face as he had felt himself being handed over into rough hands. It had been his first and only memory of her, and only by watching the families in the crowds of fair goers had he been able to name her as his mother. Sitting here now, in her home, he suddenly felt smothered. What had started as overwhelming concern over Meg's welfare had suddenly grown to include gratitude for their hospitality, shock at the woman's words, and now rage. He got up from the table and walked over to the window. Only the blizzard serving as a reminder of why he was here stopped him from walking out the door. He hung his head and spoke in a slow, careful tone. "You mean to tell me that you are my mother? You dare to admit that you were the one who covered my face and sold me into a life of humiliation and fear?"

"Erik, I hear the anger in your voice and I do not blame you for it. If you walk out that door right now, I will not hold it against you. I know how wrong I was. I knew it the moment you left my sight. You have not left my heart, Erik."

"That does not erase the scars on my back from all those beatings! That does nothing for the laughter and jeers and screams that are forever ringing in my ears or all those nights I spent locked in a cage crying out for someone, anyone to hold me!" Erik turned to face her then, and out of the corner of his eyes, he watched little Claire clutch her doll closer to her chest as she backed into her mother's arms. He felt his eyes soften then; he had no desire to instill fear into those that offered their home as a shelter. Instead, he slid into the chair closest to Meg's side, tears running down his face.

"Claire, go get the quilt off my bed." The widow quietly ordered, and the girl was quick to obey. Slowly, Erik's mother took the quilt and walked over to the sofa, where she covered Meg's shivering form. She then sat down in the only other chair, facing Erik. "It appears that we have both been lonely for the same thing. And it was all my doing. No, I cannot change what you have endured because of me. We have only the present. And right now I'm saying that I'm sorry."

"I think that before anything else is said, we should all sit down for the nice breakfast Marie has prepared. Perhaps while we're eating, we could introduce ourselves." Jean-Claude cleared his throat. Everyone moved in silent agreement, and soon they were focused on the omelets in front of them.

"To start, Erik, in case you are uncomfortable with calling me your mother, my name is Madame Jane Dupree. Your father was Robert Dupree, and he passed on some years ago." The widow broke the silence. Erik nodded, unsure of which name he preferred. "This is your sister, Marie, and her husband, Jean-Claude."

"And I'm Claire." Erik's niece spoke up, and her excitement was met with chuckles around the table. "Isn't Meg going to eat?" Claire looked toward the sofa in all her childlike concern.

"Meg's a little sleepy right now. We must let her rest." Erik shifted uncomfortably.

"Might I ask how you got caught in the blizzard?" Jean-Claude questioned.

"It's a long story, but we have been traveling all night. Perhaps after I've rested a while, I will tell it to you."

"Oh, of course! Erik, you may take the loft. Claire, go bring your things down to our room." Marie began clearing away the empty dishes.

"I don't want to be any trouble. I could sleep on the floor..." Erik began to protest.

"Nonsense. You're family, after all." His sister smiled.

It took the next two days to get Erik used to the normal sleep cycle, and on the second morning, he came down the ladder to see Meg sitting up on the sofa. "Meg!" He flew to her side and pulled her into an embrace.

"Your sister has told me the news. To think, that storm brought us here of all places!"

"Meg...I...I nearly lost you..."

"I'm here, Erik, and I always will be."

"The fact still remains that your mother was right about me not thinking things through. It was my impulsiveness that nearly laid you at death's door..." Tears slid down his face, and Meg brought her hand up to wipe them away.

"There's that self-doubt again! I'll not have it in my presence, do you hear me?" Meg smiled as she used his own words against him. He recognized them immediately, and smiled through his tears. Just then, Claire emerged from her parents' room and immediately went up to Erik. She placed the worn-out doll into his hands, and he stared at it, completely at a loss.

"This is Sylvia. She's a ballerina, and she always makes me feel better when I'm crying." Claire explained. Erik let out a heart-felt laugh, and Meg giggled with him.

"There, you see? She's done it for you, Uncle Erik!" Claire squealed in delight.

"Thank you, Claire. Did you know that Meg's a ballerina as well?" Erik had grown somewhat accustomed to his niece's innocence and curiosity, and he watched now as her eyes lit up.

"Really? Can you teach me?"

"Perhaps after breakfast, Claire." Marie had been watching the exchange from the kitchen as she made a generous stack of crepes. After setting the platter on the table, she began setting out jam and butter, and Jean-Claude soon emerged from his room.

"Ah, Meg, I see you've finally recovered." He observed before sitting at the table.

"Yes...thank you." Meg smiled as Erik helped her to her feet, and they made their way over to the table.

"Erik, before you sit down, would you mind bringing a plate over to Mama?" Marie asked, and Erik hesitated. After he had woken up later that first day, he had found his mother had returned to her bed, and, aside from telling his story to the family, he had avoided her ever since. He still did not know if he could trust her...or himself for that matter. He also feared that if he completely accepted her as his mother, she would abandon him again. "Erik, please? She has not been well...it would do her good to know that you forgive her before she..." It was the first time he had seen his sister let a tear slide down her face. In the short time that he had been there, she had shown nothing but strength and patience. With a sigh, he grasped the warm plate and brought it to his mother's bedside. He watched as her chest rose and fell with every even breath, and he noted how small she looked even on this tiny bed. He gingerly placed his hand on her shoulder, and her eyes fluttered open.

"I...brought you breakfast..." Erik set the plate on her night table, then jumped as she took hold of his hand.

"Will you sit with me, my child?" Her voice was soft and weak, and he lowered himself to the bed next to her. He would not look at her, however; instead his gaze moved around the tiny room, then stopped as he noticed a violin set up in the corner.

"You play the violin?" He asked.

"No...that was your father's. Does the excitement in your voice mean that you play?"

"Yes...living under an opera house has its benefits. Music is one of them."

"Then I want you to have it. It does nothing but gather dust. Your father would be turning over in his grave if he knew that. He played it all the time...now this tiny house seems large with silence." Erik walked over to the instrument and placed it into position. Closing his eyes, he felt the strings under his fingers, and he played a short tune. "You have your father's gift, I see." Erik did not respond as he set the violin back down. He then silently helped his mother sit up and put the plate in her lap.

"Your breakfast is getting cold." He hinted.

"Thank you for bringing it to me. I'll not keep you from your food any longer." He heard the pain in her voice as she dismissed him, but he chose to ignore it and returned to the table.

After breakfast, Meg asked Erik if she could speak to him privately. Marie and Jean-Claude brought Claire into their room so that they could talk, and Meg pulled Erik over to the sofa. "Erik, I see you've been distancing yourself from your mother."

"I just don't know how I feel about her yet. My entire childhood was yanked away from me."

"Yes, I know that, Erik. But I think the guilt she's felt served as punishment enough. You're together now. That's what matters."

"You don't understand, Meg. Your mother was there for you. And even if I do forgive her...you heard Marie. She's not well. Why should I get attached to her just so she can leave me again? It's easier this way."

"Erik, that's the most selfish thing I've ever heard. It would be easier for you, but not for her. Don't make her pass on with the knowledge that you don't love her or forgive her. Put yourself in her shoes." Erik cringed at her sharp, blunt words. *Why must you insist on being right all the time?* With a sigh, he stood and began pacing the floor. "Put yourself in her shoes," Meg had said. *Well, Erik? How would you feel if Christine hadn't accepted your apology? How would you feel if one of the most important people in your life refused to forgive you? Curse you, Meg!*

"I suppose you're right..." He finally spoke with a heavy sigh.

"Of course I am. Now go to her." Meg motioned toward the widow's closed bedroom door.

"Come with me?" Erik requested anxiously, and Meg followed him in. She stood just behind his shoulder, placing her hand on his arm as he woke up the sleeping woman. She looked up at him with a careful smile, and he knelt down. "I...I don't want to punish you any longer than you've already punished yourself. I forgive you, Mama..." The name sounded completely foreign as it made its way past his lips, and as he spoke it, he felt tears from so long ago fill his eyes. He placed his forehead on her bony arm, and she slowly placed her other hand on his head.

"Oh, my son...you have no idea how relieved I am to hear you say that!" She began weeping as well, and Meg slowly backed away, giving mother and son some privacy.

Chapter Seventeen: A Mother's Heart

Erik remained at his mother's side for several hours. The pent up tears from both of their pasts had at last dried up after the first hour. Madame Dupree then told him how she had felt so guilty that she had gone back to the fair when it was in Paris, prepared to take him back with her, but she was told that he had escaped. It was then that she had initially felt that she had given up all rights to seeing him again. Erik then explained how Antoinette had helped him hide from the authorities, but he spoke no further of Madame Giry. Instead, a bitter thought entered his mind. *If it wasn't for Antoinette, I could have gotten my life back...* But then, he remembered, if it hadn't have been for Antoinette, he would have never met Meg. "Have I lost you to your thoughts?" Madame Dupree broke the silence, and Erik shook his head.

"No, Mama...I'm still here..." he smiled, squeezing her hand gently.

"Tell me something, Erik. How long do you plan on running away from your problems?"

"I don't exactly have a choice. If I am going to start a new life, I can't let anyone hold me back."

"Did it not occur to you to give them a chance to help you start?"

"You don't understand. Antoinette wanted to keep me down there, away from Meg. She thought I didn't belong anywhere else. She thought I didn't deserve Meg." Erik got up and crossed the room. He had wanted to avoid this. He had wanted to erase Antoinette Giry from his mind for as long as possible.

"From a mother's perspective, I would think that by running away, you have only proved her point."

"Why are you doing this to me?" Tears had welled up all over again, and he didn't try to stop them.

"Do not get me wrong, Erik. I know how much you care for Meg. But I also see the distant sadness in her eyes. The bond between a mother and her child is one of the strongest in the world, and no matter how much Meg loves you, she will still love her mother and want her by her side. Erik, if you really do love Meg, you will bring her back to Paris. You will trust her to wait for you while you get your life figured out."

"Mama, I gave her that choice! She chose to come with me."

"She was probably afraid of saying the wrong thing."

"You do not know that."

"I know I don't. But I think you need to discuss this with her further." Just then, there was a light knock on the door.

"Mama's got the noon meal on the table..." Claire's soft voice called. Erik opened the door and followed his niece to the table, where Meg and Jean-

Claude were already sitting. As they ate, Erik watched Meg's face, and he could now see the distant sadness in her eyes as well. She kept smiling at him and at Claire, but he saw it. *Curses.* "Meg, will you dance for us?" Claire pleaded once the meal was done.

"I'll need some music..." Meg threw a hinting glance at Erik, and he retrieved the violin from his mother's room. At the last minute, he turned to face the elderly woman.

"Would you like to watch?"

"I would love nothing more." Carefully, Erik lifted his mother and carried her to the sofa before picking up the violin again.

"Just play anything. I'll follow you." Meg had slipped on the ballet slippers and was now standing in the middle of the floor. Erik lifted the violin to his chin and began playing a lively tune, one that matched Meg's personality. He watched her close her eyes as she leaped and twirled; surely she was in her element. When the song and dance ended, Claire led the applause enthusiastically, and as Erik looked in his mother's direction, he saw she was looking at him in a way that said "Do you really want to take her away from that?" He was thankful when Claire insisted on another one, but the doubt had returned for what would seem like a long stay.

That evening, Erik asked Meg to sit with him on the sofa. Taking a deep breath, he turned to face her. "Meg, you miss the opera don't you?"

"Of course I do. But it's a sacrifice I'm willing to make for us to be together."

"I appreciate you wanting to be brave, Meg, but I'm beginning to realize that maybe we were a bit too hasty in our actions."

"You were reunited with your family, though." Meg pointed.

"True enough. But I don't want you to lose yours." Erik watched as she hung her head.

"I don't want to lose you, though..." A tear glistened on her face, and he gently put his hand under her chin and forced her to look at him. Slowly, he brought his other hand to her face and brushed the tears away.

"I promise you, Meg, you will not lose me. My mother told me this morning that if we really love each other, whatever time we spend separated will pale in comparison to the years we'll spend together." Meg was really sobbing now, and he pulled her to him in a warm embrace. "Tomorrow I'll talk with Jean-Claude about traveling arrangements and employment opportunities that might be in the village. We'll then return to Paris and end your mother's worry. If I cannot find anything here in the village, I'll see about finding work in the city."

"Erik...what if..."

"Shh..." Erik placed his lips on the top of her head and began to hum a quiet tune. Her shoulders soon stopped shaking, although she let a few sniffles escape. "You were brave to come with me, Meg. Now I need you to be a little bit braver. Do you think you can?"

"I love you, Erik." Meg looked into his eyes.

"I love you too." Erik kissed her cheek softly before retiring to the loft for the night.

They were floating on air, or at least it seemed that way. Music came from everywhere and nowhere as they held each other close, dancing under the moonlight. Suddenly, the music stopped, and Meg laughed as she pulled away from him. He started to follow her down towards the splashing waves, but something was weighing him down. She twirled and skipped, laughing away as she seemed oblivious to him. "Where are you going, Meg?" he called out, but the waves drowned out his voice. Further and further she went, completely carefree. "Meg, come back! Meg!"

"Uncle Erik! Uncle Erik! Wake up!" He felt himself being shaken awake with tiny arms, and he sat up immediately.

"What? What is it?" The line between reality and his dream was all but faded away completely, and his thoughts instantly turned to Meg.

"It's Grandmama...Mama said to come get you..." Claire's voice sounded urgent, and yet there was a trace of fearful shakiness that proved that she was crying. Erik quickly stumbled down the ladder and flew to his mother's bedside. Marie and Jean-Claude were already there, and his sister had a steady stream of tears flowing down her face as she grasped her mother's hand.

"Erik...I need to...speak with Meg..." Jane Dupree's voice was breathless, and Erik's heart sank. He felt bolted to the floor, and Jean-Claude pushed past him to get Meg from the sofa. The dancer soon appeared in the doorway. "Please...leave us alone...I promise that I won't go just yet..." Marie let out a sob as she kissed her mother's cheek, and she pulled Erik out of the room.

"Madame Dupree?" Meg slowly walked over to the widow's bedside, questions plastered all over her face.

"Please sit, child...I won't keep you long..." Erik's mother patted the bed beside her, and Meg gingerly obeyed. "I...just want to say...that my son carries a heavy burden on his shoulders...he may not act like it, but he is...a very fragile man...may God give you...the strength...to take care of him...and to give him...all he needs..."

"I won't let you down, Madame Dupree. I promise. I'll look after him..." Meg let a few tears fall down her cheeks.

"I know you will...I know...that you will be...a daughter-in-law that I would be proud of..." Madame Dupree smiled.

Erik sat straight in the chair, not moving his gaze from his mother's door. At least, he wasn't planning to. His train of concentration was broken by little Claire climbing up onto his lap. This was the closest she had ever gotten to him, and she looked up at him with fear in her face. It wasn't fear of him, of course. He could see that it was fear of the situation around her. Slowly, he put his arms around her, and she clung to him even tighter. "What's going to happen, Uncle Erik?" She let out a whimper. Erik glanced over at Claire's parents, but Jean-Claude was too busy consoling his wife. Erik sighed and cleared his throat.

"Everything will be all right, little Claire. It might not look that way now, but everything will turn out fine." He chose his words carefully, not knowing if she understood the concept of death yet. As she continued to tremble, he decided to change the subject. "Claire, I want you to see something. Let me get it out of my bag." Claire hesitantly got off of his lap, and he leaned forward to grab his satchel. Opening it, he pulled out his music box. Holding it out to her, he wound it up and let it play. "I've had this my whole life, Claire. It always brought comfort to me when I was sad, just like your

Sylvia doll does for you. Why don't you hold onto this for a while. Just listen to the music." He set the monkey toy on the floor in front of her, and she sat down next to it, staring at the little cymbals. Just then, Madame Dupree's door opened, and Meg tearfully motioned for them to go back in. Taking a deep breath, Erik shuffled in after everyone else and went over to his mother's side.

"My children, nothing makes me happier than to have us all together again." The widow grasped onto both her children's hands, and Erik suddenly felt like he could no longer stand. Slowly, he lowered himself to kneel, and he lightly rested his head on his mother's chest. "Oh, Erik...I am only sorry that we knew each other for such a short time. Promise me that you...will look after the rest...of your family..."

"I will, Mama. I promise." Sobs now shook his body, and he made no move to stop them.

"Take care...of yourself...and of Meg..."

"Yes, Mama..." *Not yet! Don't leave me just yet!*

"I am proud...of both my children...I couldn't ask...for a better son...or a better daughter..." Madame Dupree began coughing. "I love you..." Her final words were voiced in a whisper, and Erik felt her hand go limp.

"I love you too, Mama..." Erik held her body close then, not ready to let go. Marie walked around the bed to stand behind him, and she put her hands on her brother's shoulders. "No...not yet...she can't go yet..." Erik sobbed.

"I'm so sorry, Erik...at least she knew that you loved her..." Marie's voice was shaky, and he realized he was not alone in his grief. Slowly, he let go of the widow's lifeless form and rose to his feet. He looked at

Marie as if he only now found out that he had a sister, and he felt that he had to be strong. He wrapped his arms around her, and the tiny family wept together for a good half hour.

The undertaker came at dawn. Jane Dupree's body would be stored in the funeral parlor's basement until spring, and Erik vowed that no matter what he was doing at that time, he would be there to say a final good bye. For now, all he could do was plant a final kiss on her stone cold forehead before the white sheet covered her entirely. Meg stood by his side as they watched the carriage drive away, and when it had disappeared completely down the road, he put a hand to his eyes and wept into it. "I knew this would happen, Meg...I knew that if I got attached..." As his voice faded away, Meg pulled him into a full hug.

"Erik, you are experiencing what Christine and Mama and millions of others have experienced. Your grief is normal. I know one thing, though. I know that no matter how much it hurts, Christine does not regret ever knowing her father." Erik's only response was to sob even more into her shoulder, and they held each other for several minutes before a familiar tune broke the silence. Erik glanced down to see Claire holding the monkey toy out to him, her eyes brimming with tears.

"You can have this back, Uncle Erik. You need it now." Erik managed a half-smile as he took the music box, and he knelt down to pull his niece into a hug while the tune came to a finish. Wiping his tears away, he stood back up.

"Why don't we see if your mother needs any help with breakfast?" He suggested. Claire slowly nodded in agreement, and they made their way into the kitchen. Marie was standing over the stove, tears streaming down her face. Meg slowly approached her from behind.

"I'll take care of breakfast, Marie. Why don't you just relax?"

"Thank you, Meg. I don't know what I'd do without you." Marie smiled and went into her room, closing the door behind her.

The rest of the day dragged on, with very little interaction between the five of them. Erik took over his mother's room, and behind the closed door he resorted to playing the violin to ease the pain in his heart. Jean-Claude stayed by Marie's side, whether in their room or in the kitchen, and so Meg spent the day trying to entertain Claire with a few simple dance lessons.

The next day, Marie was able to go about her normal routine, albeit with several bouts of weeping, however Jean-Claude was always there to comfort her. Erik, however, did not emerge from his mother's room, even at meal times. That evening, Meg carried a steaming plate into the room, not bothering to knock as she heard the sad violin tune. Erik did not look up at her from his seat on the bed, and Meg sat down next to him. Slowly, she put her hand on the violin, and he made no effort to stop her from setting it aside. "Erik, do not do this to yourself again. I know exactly what you are doing, and I don't want to see you go through that torture again. You'll end up neglecting to eat; instead you'll surrender to your feverish nightmares...I couldn't bear to see that happen."

"What else am I supposed to do, Meg? There's so much I have yet to ask...so much I have yet to learn...I need her still. I miss her..."

"I know, Erik, I know. I wish there was something I could say to ease your pain, but there's not. The fact is, grief can last a lifetime. But you can't shut the world out. We love you and care about you." Meg softly brushed her fingers through his hair, and he closed his eyes and leaned his head against her touch. "Please, Erik. Don't make me watch you waste away." Meg whispered before lightly kissing his scarred face. Erik wrapped his arms around her then, crying into her shoulder.

"Meg, what could I have possibly done to deserve you?" The question was rhetorical, and Meg slowly placed the plate onto his lap.

"Eat something...please?" She looked pleadingly into his eyes, and he lifted a forkful of food to his mouth. "Thank you. I'm here for you, Erik, if you'll let me." Meg patted his thigh before returning to the kitchen.

It took another three days before Erik was finally able to speak with Jean-Claude about his future. The opportunity came after the noon meal, when Marie was busy with dishes and Meg was entertaining Claire. "Tell me, Jean-Claude, what is it you do for a living?"

"I'm a traveling merchant, when the weather is warmer than it is now. Thankfully, I make enough in the other seasons for us to survive these winter months. Of course, the fact that most of my business is done near Paris helps a great deal with that."

"I see. Is there anything that this village is lacking? A teacher perhaps, or an architect?"

"No, these villagers are simple people. We rely on our own strengths and traditions to get through life." This piece of news filled Erik with disappointment, and he was deep in thought for some time before speaking again.

"How soon can arrangements be made to take Meg and I back to Paris?"

"My horses are strong and I do have a sleigh for emergencies. If you would like, I would be more than happy to take you myself. In fact, I believe a trip to Paris would do us all a bit of good. Marie, what do you say?"

"Oh, it's been so long since I last visited Paris...why, Claire hasn't even seen it!" Marie turned to face the two men.

"Then it's settled. We will leave tomorrow."

The journey to the city was nerve-wracking for Erik. He had not left on good terms with anyone, and he feared that he would be chased right back out of the city limits. Only by holding Claire on his lap and Meg beside him in the sleigh was he able to stay on this side of a complete nervous breakdown.

They opted to bypass the de Chagny mansion; Meg felt certain that Christine and Raoul had been keeping close contact with Madame Giry, and she was missing her mother most of all. And so, the second evening found them approaching the Opera Populaire. One of the first things Meg noticed was the lack of a crowd outside the front doors and the fact that there were no posters outside announcing the next production. She threw a glance at Erik, but he was equally at a loss for words. They parked outside the stable, and Erik's family followed the Parisians through the doors and into the dormitories. Meg's worries increased as she felt the lack of energy around them, as the backstage area was nearly completely empty. Finally, she heard some familiar voices coming from the stage, and she quickly rounded the corner to find her mother talking with the managers. "I'm sorry, Mama..." Her voice was quiet, and her mother whirled around to face her.

"Meg! Meg my daughter!" The ballet instructor ran into her daughter's arms, weeping.

"Are you angry with me, Mama?" Meg questioned.

"Oh, Meg...I was for some time! But something has happened, and...I'm just glad that you are here again..."

"What happened?" Meg pulled away as Erik and his family walked up behind her.

"We're ruined, that's what happened." Monsieur Andre replied.

"A few days ago, Monsieur Reyer suffered a fatal heart attack. We're now without a conductor, and therefore without an orchestra. No orchestra, no opera, we're doomed." Monsieur Firmin groaned.

"Monsieur Reyer...is...gone?" Meg's jaw dropped.

"Did we not just say that?" Andre raised a questioning eyebrow at her.

"Gentlemen, you are wrong to say that you are without a conductor." Erik spoke up. "Perhaps I can be of some assistance."

Chapter Eighteen: A Fresh Start

What in the world have I gotten myself into? Erik rubbed his aching head, although it was his ears he was more worried about. *You just had to go ahead and make that bloody promise to Carlotta, didn't you? You didn't even think it would ever come to this! Final rehearsal. It's bloody final rehearsal and she's still screeching out her notes! Me and my no-good sense* *of duty.* Biting back a snarl, Erik looked up from the orchestra pit at the Prima Dona. She was glaring at the dancers around her instead of focusing on the song. "Signora, I believe that was your cue..." Erik spoke up.

"Cue for what? How am I supposed to sing with all these people dancing around me?" Carlotta pouted.

"Signora, for the last time. This is how it is going to be tonight, so deal with it!" Erik barked.

"No! You deal with it because I will not be singing!" Carlotta stomped her feet and retreated to her posse. *Good.* Erik wanted to say. *Go ahead. Walk out. And don't let the door hit you on your way out.* But a promise was a promise, and so he had to let the managers grovel. After massaging his head once more, he looked back up at the stage again just in time to catch Meg stealing a glance at him. Erik noted how beautiful and adorable she looked in her green and white costume, and he smiled at her. She smiled back and mouthed 'I love you' before turning her attention to the La Carlotta drama unfolding. Erik didn't catch the words. All he could hear was shouting when he should be hearing singing. For a moment, he realized that the pranks he had once played on an almost regular basis had caused Monsieur Reyer to feel this frustrated. *But if Carlotta knew how to sing, I wouldn't have needed to take those actions.* Before he could think any further, Carlotta returned to the center of the stage, wiping fake tears off her face.

"Ah. You're back. May we continue?" Erik raised an eyebrow.

"Maestro..." Carlotta nodded, and after taking a deep breath, Erik motioned for the orchestra to start over.

And now let us rewind two weeks to the day they arrived and Erik made this offer. At first, the managers were reluctant, but they were quickly reminded that Erik was their only hope. And so, Erik Dupree was hired as the new orchestra conductor right then and there. It was agreed that he would wear the mask Meg had given to him whenever he was with the performers and the opera goers. Meg had gone right back into her routine of dancing and practicing, and now that Erik was there every day, she had all the more enthusiasm about it. She had quickly sent word to Christine and Raoul, who would make it a point to be there for opening night. Jean-Claude, Marie, and Claire were invited to stay as guests at the opera house for the remainder of winter, and Christine's old dressing room was fixed up as a small bedroom and living quarters(Erik made sure to bolt the mirror/door shut.) It was also decided that as soon as everyone got back into the flow of things, a new suite would be built as an upper floor on its own above the stables, where Erik would then be free to live and compose his music away from the dark caverns of his past. Until then, he would have to make do with the cellars, but knowing that it wasn't forever made it much easier. When he wasn't busy with the orchestra, he spent his days ridding himself of the many reminders of his past obsessions. The many drawings he had of Christine were bundled together and set aside as a gift. His music was carefully sorted through, and anything that had to do with Christine or her voice were immediately discarded along with the many dolls, costumes, and wax figures. He planned to move the organ and all his other instruments and music to the new suite, and soon, the future was looking bright.

There was still one matter to address...a matter to make official. He stared down at the diamond ring that he had stolen from Christine only to give to her later on...the one she had given back that fateful night of the fire. Fingering it, he thought of all that had happened between then and now. A year. It had been one year exactly. His future had been so uncertain then.

Looking back, he wanted to strangle himself for not thinking about the future more seriously. But no, the past was past, and all seemed to be forgiven. He dropped the ring into his pocket and adjusted his wig and mask. Opening night. How he was going to get through this, he had no idea. Carlotta's voice was bad enough without this other matter floating around in his mind. He had spoken with Madame Giry that morning, before final rehearsal began. It had taken some talking and a lot of listening, but finally Antoinette had embraced him with her blessing.

Erik nodded to the orchestra now, emitting confidence from his face. Raising the baton, he signaled for the music to begin. Throughout the performance, he had to keep reminding himself to ignore Carlotta at all costs, but once in a while a particularly sharp note hit his ears painfully, and he was grateful when the dancers came on. He watched Meg perform the routines flawlessly, and he sighed with relief at how perfect life was getting.

"Erik, that was brilliantly done!" He was hearing that a lot tonight it seemed, but each time he heard it, he felt it like the first. He was certainly not used to this much positive attention, especially from those who had once feared, mocked, and spread rumors about him. Part of him wanted to just grab Meg and pull her into a dark corner where he could speak with her alone, but there were far too many people standing around backstage. Finally, Madame Giry pushed her way through the crowd, and Christine and Raoul were at her heels. As if on cue, Meg slid in next to Erik and wrapped her arm around his.

"Erik, Meg, I believe you two have something to discuss with the Vicomte and his wife..." Antoinette hinted.

"Yes, I do owe you both an apology. I did not mean to worry you..."

"Neither of us did..." Meg put in, her tone of voice clearly telling Erik to stop blaming himself.

"You are forgiven." Raoul spoke up, and he shook Erik's hand.

"Madame Giry tells us that you were reunited with your family..." Christine smiled, and for a moment, Erik felt an ache in his heart at the memory of his mother.

"Yes...my sister and her daughter had to retire early tonight, but I do hope that you might meet them tomorrow."

"We wouldn't miss it." Raoul nodded, and they excused themselves to mingle with the other performers. Antoinette paused to raise a questioning eyebrow at Erik, and he subtly nodded. Madame Giry took a last look at the both of them before following the de Chagnys.

"Meg...I wish to speak with you...alone..." Erik cleared his throat while inwardly wondering how butterflies had gotten themselves trapped in his stomach.

"Oh? What about?"

"Come with me..." Erik grasped her hand and led the dancer away from the crowds and into the stables. He motioned for her to take a seat in one of the carriages.

"Are we going somewhere?" Meg wore a puzzled look on her face, causing Erik to smile before removing the mask.

"That's entirely up to you. I would like very much..." There were those butterflies again, only they had multiplied. By a hundred. "If you would be my bride." Erik knelt down on one knee and removed the ring from his pocket.

"It's about time you asked!" Meg jumped down into his arms, and he lifted her up and swung her around before planting a kiss on her lips. He then grasped her left hand and slid the diamond ring onto her finger, and he could have sworn that there wasn't a happier man in all the world than he was at that moment.

"What is this?" A certain Italian diva stormed into Erik's office. *Leave it to Carlotta to ruin such a perfect day...* Erik hesitantly looked up from the music sheets spread across his desk. Carlotta threw a piece of paper on top of the stack. *Obviously I'm not going to get any work done...* With a sigh, Erik read the notice, trying to hide a smirk.

"It appears to be announcing auditions for a lead soprano. 'Willing to train the right voice.'"

"I can read, Monsieur! It appears *you* are blind because you already *have* a lead soprano! 'Ave you forgotten our little agreement?"

"Madame, I am merely taking precautionary measures, as you are constantly quitting at the drop of a hat. This is just for back up, that is all."

"No it is *not* all! Who's idea was this?"

"If you must know, it was decided upon by myself and the managers. It just isn't fair for a single person to hold up an entire production."

"So I am just supposed to stand back and allow myself to be replaced by some amateur?"

"Madame, as I said, this is simply a precautionary measure. As long as you don't threaten to quit, you may sing. Just don't expect us to lay the world at your feet every time you aren't happy here. Now if you don't mind, I have work to do." Erik set the flier aside and began writing again.

"This is not over, Maestro!"

"Are you still here?" Erik kept his eyes on the sheet music, and when the door slammed hard enough to shake the walls, he let out a chuckle.

Throughout the rest of the winter, Erik busied himself with training Alyce to be Carlotta's understudy while Antoinette and Meg gave Claire more dancing lessons. All too soon, it was the evening before Erik's family went back to their village, and they had just finished a private late-night supper with Erik, Meg, and Antoinette in the former dressing room. It had been a particularly long day, between rehearsals and packing, and little Claire let out a huge yawn as soon as her plate was empty. "Come, Claire, it's time for bed. We must leave early tomorrow." Marie smiled.

"Is Uncle Erik coming with us?" The little girl asked sleepily, and Erik felt a lump forming in his throat.

"I'll be staying here this time, Claire." He allowed his regret to seep into his voice.

"But I don't want to go without you!" Claire all of a sudden regained enough energy to run into his arms, and he felt a few tears in the corners of his eyes as he held his niece close.

"It won't be forever. I'll be coming to visit in a month or two."

"That's right, and then in the summer we'll be coming back here for the wedding." Marie spoke up.

"What's a wedding?" Claire sniffled.

"It's when Meg becomes a part of our family." Marie smiled.

"Yes...she'll become your Aunt Meg." Erik added.

"I never had a aunt before..." Claire yawned again, and Erik stood up with her in his arms.

"May I?" He asked his sister, who nodded. Erik gently brought his niece over to her cot and lowered her to the mattress. Slowly, he pulled the blankets over her tiny form and placed a soft kiss on her forehead. "Sleep well, little Claire." He smiled.

Behind him, Antoinette had approached Marie. "Your daughter learns quickly. I can already tell that she has a wonderful talent in dancing."

"Thank you. I appreciate you teaching her...you too, Meg."

"Claire is young yet, but I promise you that she will always have a spot waiting for her in the ballet."

"Oh, thank you, Antoinette! Only time will tell, but I am sure she will love that." Marie flashed a beaming smile at the older woman.

Meg sat back in her seat, watching Erik's interactions with his young niece. Her heart nearly melted at the signs of his soon-to-come tears; who knew that such a little girl would have such an effect on the former Phantom of the Opera? And then she had heard her mother's offer to Marie, and she thought of how wonderful it would be. To have Erik's family in his life again would have been unthinkable just a year ago, and now she couldn't imagine life any other way. They had welcomed him back with open, loving arms, and hadn't judged him in any way. It had been a natural, smooth transition, and it never would have happened without everything else taking place before. She couldn't help feeling thankful for all of it...Erik's nightmares, Fredrique's attack, the lessons, her visit with Christine...it all made sense now, and yet all of it had caused her so much pain at the time.

"Meg?" Meg blinked and shook her head. Erik was looking down at her with concern in his eyes.

"I'm sorry...I was just...thinking..."

"You look tired as well. Shall I walk you to your door?" He extended his hand, and she took it. They bid good night to Erik's family before stepping out into the corridor.

"That was very sweet of you, you know." Meg smiled up at him.

"What was?"

"You tucking Claire in for the night. If I didn't know any better, I would say that you are getting soft."

"Yes, well, you started it. I can't believe I was able to treat you so roughly when we first met." They had reached her door, and he now pulled her into a kiss. "Get some sleep, my stubborn sweet dancer."

'You too, my stubborn sweet genius." Meg kissed him again before disappearing through the doorway.

Erik stared at the closed door and sighed. Summer couldn't come soon enough.

Chapter Nineteen: Final Passages

In the days that followed Erik's return from his mother's burial, he spent every free second he had to oversee the construction on the new suite. Surely, if he wasn't busy with the orchestra, he would be doing every single task himself, just to be sure every last detail was just right. The builders soon learned that when he stopped in front of the particular piece they were working on, he was going to find something wrong with it. Oh, but Meg certainly did her share to attempt to distract him, asking him questions about the wedding plans and such, but it was no use. His mind was always wandering. Finally, the suite was finished, and Erik did a final walk through. He had brought his music and instruments as far as the stables, and the workers had done the rest to put them in their rightful place. All other furnishings had been purchased on Erik's rare days off. The suite consisted of a large sitting room with an adjoining library and office. There was a separate room for his music and artwork, a kitchenette, and two bedrooms aside from the master bedroom. Erik would have loved to have his own bed moved up from the caverns, but it had been impossible. Instead, he had scoured every furniture shop in Paris and the surrounding villages, questioning every wood carver he could find, until he finally found one that would meet his request. The bed he purchased had been hand-carved in several pieces which could be fit together easily once inside the suite. It resembled a much larger version of his gondola, with music notes carved in the sides and painted in gold. The headboard was carved in the shape of a heart, as was the mattress. The linens were of crimson red, and the canopy curtains were of black lace.

The workers stood in the doorway now, watching anxiously as Erik made his inspection. Finally, he turned to them and nodded, and they let out a collective sigh of relief. "You have all done well. Now if you'll follow me down to my office, I will see that you get paid." When he reached his office, however, Monsieur Firmin was waiting for him.

"Pardon me, Monsieur, but we have a small crisis on our hands."

"Crisis?" Erik raised an eyebrow. "Monsieur, tomorrow is opening night. There is no such thing as a 'small' crisis this close to opening night."

"Yes, well, it seems our leading soprano has a nasty cold."

"You can be sure I had nothing to do with that." Erik began shuffling through the stacks of bills on his desk before handing them out to the workers.

"No one said you did. It's just that she insists on singing still."

"Is she out of her mind? Is she *trying* to infect the entire cast?" Erik whirled around to face the manager.

"She refuses to allow Alyce to replace her." Firmin shrugged.

"That does it. Promises or not, that just does it!" Erik flew down the corridor to Carlotta's dressing room, from which he could hear loud cough's and sneezes between screeching notes. *Just when I thought she couldn't possibly sound any worse...* Erik gritted his teeth before knocking.

"Who is it?" The Italian's hoarse voice sang out.

"Madame Carlotta, get out here this instant!" Erik roared in response.

"No I will not, Monsieur because I am getting my costume fitting done! You will have to wait until rehearsal to hear me sing!" *Amazing. Even with a cold she's still so very much Carlotta!* Erik began grinding his teeth and snarling at the door.

"Erik?" Meg's sudden voice behind him caused him to nearly jump out of his skin. "Erik, I know that look on your face. What is it?" *Leave it to Meg to break through and soften my heart.* With a sigh, Erik pulled his fiance down the hall.

"The diva's a disaster, that's what! I know what I promised, Meg, but I've had it! I have to fire her! I must! Let someone else deal with her!"

"What has she done now?" Meg placed a soothing hand on his arm.

"She's trying to get the whole cast ill just to keep Alyce from singing in her place! She's a disaster, I tell you!" *I'm going to lose my mind any second. I just know it!* Meg rolled her eyes.

"Tell the managers to hold an emergency meeting in your office. I'll get my mother to join you." Before Erik could say another word, Meg was gone.

Ten minutes later, Erik sat behind his desk, facing the managers, Madame Giry, and Meg. He had already made his opinion clear to them, and was now attempting to calm down while he awaited someone...anyone...to speak. Finally, Monsieur Andre spoke up. "Tell me one thing, Erik. Mademoiselle Alyce...is she ready?" Erik's face fell. He hadn't thought of that. *Curses!*

"Not...quite..." He reluctantly admitted.

"Not to mention she is a bit young for the part." Antoinette pointed out.

"But there's no one else! Perhaps if we can keep everyone a safe distance from her..." Monsieur Firmin panicked.

"Impossible, Monsieur. I simply cannot move the dancers around on such short notice." Madame Giry argued.

"I'll sing it." Meg's voice was so quiet among the tension in the room that for a moment Erik wasn't sure she had actually spoken.

"Meg, are you sure? You know the songs?" He raised an eyebrow, almost too afraid to hope that she wasn't deceiving them.

"Of course I know them. And yes, Erik, I am sure. It's been quite some time since I last sang a solo."

"Then it's settled. Now the question is, what do we do with Carlotta?" Andre questioned.

"I told you. Fire her." Erik's voice was just above a growl.

"And have you arrested? You forget you made a promise to her, Erik." Antoinette reminded him.

"What were the exact terms of that agreement?" Firmin leaned forward in his chair.

"I would not interfere with her voice, she would drop the charges." Erik recalled.

"And were the charges dropped?" Firmin looked to Antoinette then, who had overseen the agreement in all its proceedings.

"From what I can recall, Piangi was recorded as having a freak accident, and the case was closed."

"Well then, it appears our Italian diva has nothing to bargain with." Erik grinned.

"Wait just a minute. We cannot just fire La Carlotta. It would be bad publicity. No, no...just won't do at all." Monsieur Andre argued. "Think of the headlines. 'World famous soprano La Carlotta fired from the Opera Populaire after coming down with a common chest cold.' The public would never forgive us."

"Oh, and I suppose it would be better if the world reads 'Opera Populaire cancels all shows due to cold epidemic throughout the cast'?" Firmin retorted.

"Silence!" Erik all but roared.

"What if a doctor was to tell her that if she sings tomorrow night, she would never be able to sing again?" Meg broke through the tension once again.

"I suppose it's worth a try. But if she refuses to listen to him...if she even thinks of stepping anywhere near that stage..." Erik let his tone of voice finish the threat, and as everyone nodded in agreement, the meeting was adjourned.

Later that day, not even Carlotta's devotees would stay in her dressing room when the doctor came. Instead, practically the entire cast and crew stood outside her door, snickering amongst themselves at the constant screams and Italian insults. "Who are you and what are you doing here? I'll have you know that you are dealing with..."

"Please, Madame, stop talking and let me check your throat!"

"Mah throat is fine, Monsieur! Now I will ask you to leave!" There was another fit of sneezing before what sounded like a shoe was thrown at the door.

"There now you see? You can't even talk now, let alone sing! I'm recommending that you spend some time away from the opera house until your cold clears up."

"Yes, but no because you cannot tell me what to do! MAHTHA!" Carlotta's voice, although just above a whisper, was loud enough to cause those closest to the door to back away.

"Signora please. This is for the best. Spend a week or two in the country, and then come see me at my office. That will be all." With that, the door opened, and the crowd quickly dispersed. Before the door could be closed behind the doctor, another shoe flew through the doorway. The doctor approached Carlotta's mother and relayed his instructions.

"I'll pack her bags right away. Thank you."

"Uh, while you're in there, Signora, would you be so kind as to retrieve the costume for Meg?" Monsieur Firmin spoke up. The elder Italian woman grinned weakly before gingerly entering the dressing room.

"Meg, you look lovely." Erik kissed his fiance's hand. The opera was about to begin, but he did not want to miss the chance of wishing Meg luck before the show started.

"Thank you, Erik. You look handsome as well." Meg smiled. She wore a pale blue dress with white trim, and her hair was one long braid.

"You're the one they'll be looking at."

"You'd best get on out there. I can't sing without music."

"My dearest Meg, singing *is* music." Erik smirked before pulling her into an embrace. "Sing well, my Angel of Light." He whispered. Meg planted a kiss on his jaw, and he made his way to the orchestra pit. *Is it summer yet?*

This is torture. *Who came up with this stupid tradition anyway?* It was the day before the wedding, and Erik had been told that he wasn't allowed to see Meg until the ceremony. Instead, his fiance was off somewhere with Antoinette, Christine, Marie, and Claire, and Erik was stuck in the opera house. Raoul and Jean-Claude were there to keep him company, but his mind was only on Meg. "Erik, you really must stop pacing. You're making us dizzy." Raoul spoke up.

"I'll pace if I want to!" Erik growled.

"Oh, cheer up, Erik. You'll see her soon enough. Why don't we finish moving your things into your new suite?" Jean-Claude suggested. "Antoinette said that they've got Meg's things all in trunks, ready to move as well."

"I suppose we could do that." Erik sighed.

"Come on, then." Raoul led the way into Erik's office.

Everyone was standing now, which meant Meg was about to walk down the aisle. Erik was almost too afraid to look. *What if this is a dream? What if it all just disappears and I'm back in the caverns, dying? Breathe, Erik. This is real. You're going to miss it if you don't look. This is your only chance...Oh, she's beautiful. I* *don't deserve this. No way do I deserve this. I'm the Creature of Darkness. She's coming closer...that smile is more precious than all the diamonds in the world. Take her hand, Erik. Smile. Breathe. Listen.*

"Before we begin, Erik has requested that he be allowed to sing a song in honor of his bride." The priest announced, and Erik nodded to the organist before singing a brand new song.

I'm melting. *Oh that voice. It's a good thing Erik is holding my hands, otherwise I'll slip away into a puddle. How can anyone fear that handsome face? How can anyone ignore that voice? And those eyes...they used to be so sad. Now...oh, Erik, I love you too! Did I speak? I think I just spoke. I must have, for he's lifting my veil.* Meg lifted her chin to bring her lips closer to his, and the guests stood to welcome Monsieur and Madame Erik Dupree with open arms.

Chapter Twenty: Epilogue

"You may come in now, Monsieur." The midwife opened the bedroom door. Erik had ceased pacing as soon as he had heard the baby's first cry. It was a little over a year after the wedding. Erik had at first been completely terrified of the prospect of having children. He was still very terrified. Yet Meg had pointed out how well he had interacted with little Claire, insisting that it was a good sign that he would make a wonderful father.

"That's not what concerns me. What if...my face..."

"Your face is very handsome. And no matter what our children look like, we will love them the same. Stop worrying so much." Meg had caressed his scarred face lovingly before bringing her lips to his.

That was nine months ago. Now, Erik took a deep breath before stepping into the bedroom. He immediately went to Meg's side. Her face was covered in sweat and tears, and her golden locks were in a tangled circle beneath her head. He had heard her screaming, and he would have crashed through the door had Antoinette, Christine, and Raoul not been there to hold him back. Yet he could see in her face that her tears of pain had quickly turned to tears of joy. She weakly took his hand in hers and gave it a gentle squeeze. "It's a girl." She whispered. The midwife's apprentice then laid the tiny bundle in Meg's arms, and Meg instinctively started to feed her. "What shall her name be?"

"Jane. Jane Audrey Dupree." Erik swallowed a lump in his throat as he thought of his mother.

"I like it. Hello, Jane." Meg smiled down at the baby, and Erik looked on, sitting stiffly in the chair. *Is this real?* Suddenly he couldn't breathe. He crossed the bedroom and stared out the window at the stable yard.

What was it like, to be needed? He remembered when he had first asked himself that question. He recalled that first time Meg had used his chest as a pillow and his shirt as a handkerchief. Back then, he could have easily brushed off the feeling and ignored the moment. Now, he had a family. *A family.* A wife and a daughter who would need him always. The thought still terrified him. This was a whole new experience for him, and yet he wouldn't trade it for anything.

Later that night, Erik entered the bedroom, thankful that the crowds had finally left after taking their first peek at the baby. He had eventually escaped to his office; there was only so much attention he could take. Now, he crept through the darkness to the bed where Meg slept. Baby Jane was in her arms, just beginning to whimper. Unwilling to allow his wife to be disturbed, Erik gingerly lifted his daughter and held her in the moonlight. The baby girl was perfectly healthy, and Erik sighed with relief as her whimpers did not grow any louder. He sat down in one of the chairs, holding the baby to his shoulder and gently stroking her back. "You have your mother's beauty, little Jane. You have no reason to fear. You'll soon grow up into a beautiful young lady and grace the stage with your presence. And you'll never be alone, little one. Never alone."

Story Two: A Gentle Touch

I was twenty-four when we first met. By now, my face had outgrown my current mask, and so I began the process of making a new one...or at least, a plaster mold. While it was drying, I played my violin down by the lake's edge. As the music filled me and left me, I found my gaze lowering to my reflection in the water. I scowled and sighed. This was my life, my future. I put more volume into my playing, as if I could scare my face away instead of it being in control.

But then a new reflection appeared behind me—the reflection of five-year-old Marguerite Giry. I had scoffed when Antoinette told me that name—so long for such a little girl. And so I had always called her Little Giry in my mind.

Only her reflection was here—*she* was here—and my face was bare... In a split second, I set my violin down and raised my hand to the right side of my face, whirling around to face her. "Little Giry...what are you doing here?" Any anger I would have felt toward any other intruder melted then as she looked up at me with big brown eyes, and I found myself instead concerned.

"I was exploring." She did not sound afraid. Perhaps she had not seen.

"That is very dangerous. Where is your mother?"

"Upstairs." *Did this girl* ever *blink?* I sighed.

"Then let us get you back to her. She's probably worried." I reached down with my left hand to take hers, but she reached up with her left hand toward my right. I touched her right hand gently, but she kept reaching persistently.

"I want to see."

"Why?"

"Please?" Still, she had not blinked, and so I did extra blinking for her. In a state of utter shock, I found myself kneeling down to her level, allowing her to move my hand aside. Slowly, she touched my deformity, her fingers tracing each wrinkle and bump. "How did you get it?"

"I...don't know. I've always had it." I swallowed back the lump in my throat, every ounce of my energy being used to fight back my tears. Her fingers kept wandering, and I was frozen. After what seemed like the longest time, she gently brushed her lips against my cheek, pulling back and smiling.

"I like it."

"Y—you do?" At this, she nodded.

"It's different. I like different."

"Why?" *And furthermore, why am I acting the curious child and she the adult?*

"Because if everyone looked the same, I wouldn't recognize anyone." At this I managed to let out a small laugh.

"You would still be able to recognize me, Little Giry, if my right cheek matched my left."

"But I wouldn't like it."

"You wouldn't?" Her response was to shake her head. "Why?"

"My doll."

"Y—what about it?"

"*Her*."

"Very well, what about her?"

"She's missing an eye and her dress is torn, and she smells funny. But I don't want a new one."

"Oh?"

"Uh uh. A new doll would be nicer-looking and prettier-smelling, but she wouldn't be mine. My doll was with me when I was sick or scared, and I've told her all my secrets. I love her cause she doesn't make fun of me or walk away when I try to talk. She's not busy like Mama and she's always there when I need her. Why are you crying?" I immediately wiped at my tears, not realizing just how much I was sobbing.

"It...it's nothing, Little Giry. As it turns out, I have something like that." I slowly stood and made my way to my bedchamber, retrieving the monkey toy I had brought with me as I fled from the fair. I turned around to return to her, but she was right behind me. *Curse those ballerinas being light on their feet!* I slowly knelt down next to her and handed my monkey to her.

"What's his name?"

"He doesn't have one."

"He's gotta have a name! My doll's name is Suzanne."

"Well, what would you name him?"

"Nuh uh. You have to name him or he's not yours."

"Very well...how about...Maestro?" At that, she grinned.

"I like it." She handed him back, and I set him down on the bed. "That's why I like your face, Monsieur. It shows how much you were loved. Suzanne is all worn out and disfigured cause I love her so much...maybe God loves you so much that He held you a little longer." Without skipping a beat, she scurried back to the lake and picked up my violin. Placing it in my hands, she climbed onto my lap. "Can you play some more?"

"Very well...one song, and then I'll bring you upstairs."

"Okay..." She snuggled closer, and I swallowed another lump before playing once again.

Story Three: Never Alone: The Prequel

Author's Note: This story is written in alternating first person. The first chapter is Erik's perspective, the next is Antoinette's, the third is Erik's, etc. Any changes will be clearly noted.

Chapter One: Erik's First Night

I close the vent behind me and turn around. I am in a room filled with candles. *What is this place?* I do not have time to ponder. The dancing girl...Antoinette, was it?...is in the doorway. She grabs my hand and pulls me down a hallway and through several doors before we finally reach a set of spiral stairs. She has a torch in her hand, and I must hurry to follow her down into the darkness. She starts going on about how these caverns were used in the Revolution, but I cannot pay attention to that. All I can think about is what I have just done. *He had it coming. It was your life or his.*

We have reached the bottom of the stairs now, and we are trapped. The light from the torch reveals an entire lake in the underground caverns. *Is this it? Have you brought me here to die?* Antoinette points out a worn out wooden thing that must have been a boat once. It floats, nonetheless, and I wait for her to step in. "This is as far as I go. I will return with some food and clothes. Wait here." She does not wait for me to protest. She leaves me alone in the darkness, and all I can hear are her footsteps fading and the occasional squeak of a rat. *It's okay. I'm used to rats. Rats don't care if you're the Devil's Child.*

While I wait for the dancer to return, my thoughts wander to the others. Do they miss me? *I doubt it.* Most ignored me. A few were kind enough to answer my questions and teach me a thing or two about whatever piqued my curiosity at the moment, but I could tell. They'd rather I not exist. *Do they miss* him *then?* A bitterly sour taste comes to my mouth as I think of that filthy scum of a man who once called himself my master. If I had had time, I really would have given him what he deserves. Namely his whipping stick broken over his head. I feel myself smirk at the thought.

At last, I see the torch light come bouncing down the stairs, announcing her return. She tosses me a cloth sack, very similar to the one I am wearing now. "It's not much, but it will have to do for now. I'll be bringing more each week, so be sure to meet me in this very spot." She points out a long pole leaning against the wall. I assume it's use is to guide the boat through the waters.

"Light?" I point to the torch.

"Very well. I think I can find my way back." I can tell that she is hinting at something. Namely me walking her back so she's not alone in the darkness. *But what if I'm caught?* I throw the sack into the boat and step in. "Good night, then. I'll see you back here in a week." *How long is a week?* I really should ask her, but she is gone already. Once again alone in the darkness, I push the boat through the water. The caverns are much larger than I thought. I remain close to the walls, moving the torch around in order to get a better look. The air is damp and cold around me, yet I can hardly breathe under my sack. Slowly I pull it off of my head. There's no one to see me now. No one to scream, laugh, and jeer. No one to hit me and chain me in a cage. No one.

I float around a corner. The torch reveals a fair-sized platform along half of the wall. It looks dry enough. I land the boat and step out. Yes, this will make a decent home. For how long, I do not know. I retrieve the sack Antoinette gave me and pull out a loaf of bread, a shirt, and a blanket. Not knowing how long a week is, I force myself to only take a nibble of the bread before placing it back in the sack. I set the torch on the floor and lay the blanket out near it. Finally warm, I curl up and drift off into sleep...a sleep that is not without its fair share of nightmares.

Chapter Two: On Antoinette's Mind

The boy is waiting impatiently at the bottom of the stairs. I told him a week, didn't I? He is wearing the shirt I found in the prop room. It fits him well. He is still wearing the sack over his head. "Where were you?" He asks, and even with the sack covering all but his eyes, I can feel the heat from his glare.

"I told you I would be back in a week." I hand over the bag I filled with a few more clothes and a week's worth of food.

"That means nothing to someone who spent his life in a cage." I inwardly kick myself. *Of course!* I do not have time to apologize. He is pawing through the bag. "I need wood. Tools as well."

"I will be sure to bring them next time." I want to scold him for his lack of manners, but I quickly remember how sheltered he has been. "Will there be anything else?"

"Whatever you think of will be fine." His tone is dismissive, as if he is eager for me to leave.

"I can get you a new mask if you'd like. That sack looks stifling." It is a sensitive topic, particularly for just our second meeting, but it had to be asked. I feel him glaring at me again, and it is several minutes before he replies.

"I can make my own with the right materials."

"I'll see that you get them then. I suppose I'll see you in a week?"

"Good bye then." With nothing else to say, he gets back in his boat and pushes off, not taking one look back at me.

The week passes slowly. Between practices, my mind is on the masked boy. He has not told me his given name, even after I told him mine. Perhaps he has none, or perhaps it has been so long that he has forgotten it. I refuse to call him by his stage name, however. Never in all my life have I heard anything so cruel. Of course, when I was younger, there were a few drunken fathers in my neighborhood who took all their rage out on their children. I am thankful that I was sent to the opera house when I was six; although my father was never like that, I could see that my mother hated the thought of me bearing witness to the cruelty.

Perhaps it is because of the pain and humiliation that the boy does not trust me with his name yet. Part of me warns that I should not get too attached; dancing is my top priority. However, I chose to be his only link to the outside world. I did not have much time to think about what I was doing. I just knew that it was right.

Still, he needs a name. I have two sacks this time as I descend the spiral staircase, and I am shocked when I see him approaching without the boat. He is completely soaked through; I can only guess that he swam his way to the stairs. "I hope you brought wood this time," he sputters. I really must teach this boy some manners.

"Yes, I did. I also found some scraps of leather for your mask."

"That will do for now, I suppose."

"I cannot read your mind, you know. Just tell me what you need." I am growing impatient, but I hold it in. He cannot help the way he was brought up.

"The leather will do for now, as I said. It would be pointless for me to make anything permanent just yet."

"May I ask you something?"

"You just did." *Clever boy, this one.*

"Do you have a name?" He hesitates for the longest time, and I can feel him studying my face.

"You mean besides the 'Devil's Child'?"

"Don't say that! That's not a proper name for anyone!"

"Many people would say otherwise." He lets out a long sigh. "I seem to recall the name Erik."

"Pleased to meet you, Erik." I extend my hand, and he stares at it. "You're supposed to shake it." He is slow in doing so. As our eyes meet, I see so much in his. It causes me to wonder how he had ended up in the fair in the first place. He cannot be more than one or two years younger than I, and he has been so sheltered from the world, yet his eyes show that he has had to grow up much too fast. I want to question him further, but the words don't come. That subject is best left for some other time, I realize. "I'll be bringing some candles and such next time. It's far too dark down here, and I apologize for not thinking of that sooner."

"Darkness suits me just fine, though I suppose a few candles would be alright."

"Will there be anything else?"

"If I think of anything, I'll let you know." He turns to go back into the lake. I watch him toss the sacks over his thin shoulders; the water must not be as deep as I suspected, as he is able to wade through it. All too soon, darkness swallows him, and I must return to the dorm room before I am missed.

Months have passed. Each week, I have met him twenty minutes before curfew at the bottom of the stairs, and each week his list has grown longer. Erik has grown more and more accustomed to his surroundings and has accepted that the caverns are his new home. He has also become more comfortable in bossing me around, as if he owns the place. I try to teach him manners, and some he has started to stick to. Others, such as saying 'please' and 'thank you', he completely ignores, and I have given up trying to explain them to him.

Part of me is curious as to how he has made a home for himself in all that darkness, and occasionally he looks at me as if to ask if I want to join him in the boat. These looks always come after a moment of hesitation, as if he's trying to be polite as I have taught him. I can see that he really doesn't want my company, and I am still fearful of what lies beyond the lake.

His mask was finished a week after I had given him the leather material, and it covers only the right half of his face. I am now able to see more of his sadness, more of his impatience when I talk too much, and I can even see when he occasionally smirks if I show any sign of fear.

Mind you, I did not plan on showing my fear. When does one? It happened, just the same, one particular time I ventured down the stairs. A very large spider decided to perch on my shoulder on my way down, and only after I greeted Erik did it decide to show itself to me. I screamed, of course, and brushed it off onto the stone floor. "Scared of a little spider, are we?" Erik smirked for the first time. I chose not to respond. I would not give him the satisfaction. He then bent over and picked the spider up, allowing it to crawl across his arm. Slowly, he brought his arm toward me. I responded by dropping the sacks at his feet and running back up the stairs. His laughter echoed behind me, and he has teased me about it ever since. Typical boy.

His annoying teasing aside, Erik shows almost no emotion outside of bitterness. Dancing has always cheered me up, but he does not seem to be ready to learn. His security seems to come from his mask, the darkness, and the little monkey toy he brought from the fair. I remember how before the "show" began, he sat in his cage with the monkey, placing cymbals on its cloth hands, and banging them together. The simplest music, but it was music nonetheless. I wonder if he can hear the music that seems to always fill the opera house. I do not ask him, however, for if I show the tiniest bit of curiosity, it might come across as me wanting to see where he lives.

Only by the list of items that he gives me each week am I able to guess what he does down there. He is always asking for books, paper, and various writing utensils. Wood and other building materials are also always in demand. I give him what I can find, but I do not want to cause a shortage of supply in the opera house either. I usually turn to the supply of discarded props and costumes stored behind the stables. Whenever I bring Erik one of these unexpected items, I always fear that he will be angry that it isn't exactly what he asked for. Instead, he always studies each item with a raised eyebrow for the longest time before he nods in approval.

On one occasion, the orchestra was surprised with a donation of brand new instruments, and I managed to salvage quite a few discarded small instruments, including a violin. The next week, I found that the seemingly ancient organ had been taken apart and discarded. *Perhaps Erik can find a use for the old wood and metal pipes,* I thought, and it took quite a few secret trips between the stables and the staircase before it was finally delivered. I watched Erik's face that night. He said absolutely nothing as he placed the parts into his boat. He did not even ask what it had been, nor did he wait for me to explain anyway. He quickly disappeared into the darkness with the first boat load of parts, and I chose that moment to slip away until the next week.

Chapter Three: Erik's Music

  My first year beneath the opera house has been productive, once I got used to my surroundings. Between visits from Antoinette, I began exploring the many caves in my new home. One of my first discoveries was an underground stream filled with fish. Using tiny lassos, I am able to catch them quite easily. Part of me wanted to tell the dancer of this discovery, so she wouldn't bring more food than I needed. But when one has spent all that time being fed nothing but stale bread and water, he learns to appreciate any extra morsels he can get.

  My next big discovery was a cavern located directly beneath what must be the stage. I feel so drawn to the music I can hear that I spend every spare moment just standing there and listening to it. Music has been my escape for as long as I can remember; how convenient for my rescuer to bring me to such a place as an opera house! And then she surprised me with all those beautiful instruments one week...I could not speak. Those tiny cymbals I had for my monkey toy were my only instruments aside from my voice. Never could I have dreamed of ever owning anything more. And yet here it was, a whole pile of them for the taking.

I did not linger. I would not let her see the weakness in my face.

I set to work right away restoring the instruments. Most of the smaller ones were still in good condition. The organ was my biggest challenge. It was easy to figure out where each piece went, and soon I had it complete and on the highest platform in my living quarters. When my fingers first touched the keys of the massive instrument, I felt something click inside me. The music flowed through the caverns, echoing off the walls, and for once I did not care if anyone heard. From that first note on, music has quickly become my main focus. I do not play any song in particular, mainly because I do not know any. I play whatever I am feeling at the time.

At one point when Antoinette delivered a few books to me, one stuck out at me. It's pages were not filled with words, they were filled with hundreds of black dots and lines. She must have seen my puzzled expression. "I thought you might like to have it...for your instruments..."

"What for? It's nonsense!"

"It's music." For a moment, her eyes filled with pain. "Each dot is a note...each note matches a key on the organ..."

"How can you tell which one it goes to?" I know how ignorant I must have sounded then, but at the time, curiosity was getting the better of me.

"It's hard to explain when I don't have an instrument in front of me...Besides, I'm a dancer, not a musician."

"So what use do I have for this?" I tossed the music book on the ground. After a moment's hesitation, Antoinette bent down and picked it back up.

"I know someone who could teach you. I just don't know how it would work...he's new this season, Monsieur Reyer. He's the conductor..."

"When you figure it out, you may return this to me. Until then, it would do nothing but clutter up my caves." She looked as though she might comment on my possessive tone, but then she stopped herself. "If there's nothing else, I wish to return to my music." I was in my boat before she had any chance to speak. As I floated back to my living quarters, I was pleased to hear only silence behind me.

It took her a month to figure out my music lessons. Monsieur Reyer had apparently been more than pleased to teach a new musician. He only hesitated for a moment when he heard my list of demands. I copied the organ keys onto several sheets of paper, and through Antoinette I requested that he label it with the name of each note. He was quick to follow through, and he even included an example of each note on a staff, just as they appear in the music book. After all this was done, I only needed to meet with the conductor a few times. When I did, I made sure to remain hidden in the shadows of the orchestra pit while he stood off at a distance to hear me play. The lessons were at night, of course, and only an hour long. Once I got the basics down, I simply stopped asking Antoinette to arrange the lessons. Instead, I had her return the music book to me. The songs it contained I found to be beautiful, however I missed making my own music. And so, after receiving more paper from Antoinette, I started composing my first song. The tune is simple and at a much quicker pace than I usually play. It is the lyrics that came from deep inside me. I thought of my mask for inspiration, mixed with my life in the traveling fair. Once we held a party called a Masquerade, and it was then that I learned how to make different kinds of masks. I remember attending this party and laughing bitterly inside. Here all these people were, doing what I do every day by hiding behind a mask. They thought it as all fun and games. I find it a necessity. It was that bitter sense of humor towards the whole thing that wrote the lyrics for me.

As soon as the song was complete, I sent a copy of it with Antoinette to give to Monsieur Reyer. He must have loved it, as he sent no comment or criticism.

Antoinette is later than usual this week. She finally appears with two sacks and a small metal box. "You'd better have a good reason for your tardiness," I growl, although I cannot take my eyes off of the box.

"I brought you something extra. You never said when your birthday is, and it has been a year after all..." She hands me the box, and I turn it over in my hands, examining it.

"Well, what is it?" My impatience is met with a wide grin, and I let her take the box again. She turns something in the back, and music begins to play. With each repeat, the song gets slower and slower, until it stops. "Bring plenty of metal next time." I order. I must make one of these for my song. I can place my monkey toy on top; the cymbals suddenly seem quite simple compared to all the other instruments I play. As the plan forms in my mind, I feel that this week will pass much slower than all the rest.

Chapter Four: Changes for Antoinette

It's been three years since I delivered the instruments to Erik. Before then, he would accuse me of being late, to a point where I make it my mission to be on time. Now it seems that every once in a while, he is the one who makes me wait. Oh, he'll never admit it of course. "No, you're the one who is early," he'll say.

There is no point in arguing. He has made those dark caverns his kingdom, and whatever he says becomes law. I fear that to defy him too much would certainly end in death. I have seen him do it before, and now that he must be around thirteen, he can only be even more dangerous than he was before.

It appears that he is expanding his kingdom, for I have noticed some tools being left on one step in particular. I question Erik about it, and all he says is that it will be a trap for anyone who dares to venture down into his home. "Well, thank you for warning me." I try to match the sarcasm he sometimes uses. He does not reply.

Several weeks pass, and at one point he shows up with his arm in a sling. He says nothing aside from "In the future, it would be wise for you to remember which step the trap is on." It is a rarity for our conversations to stray from the routine of him listing his wants and needs. When it does, it always amazes me as to how intelligent this boy really is. Perhaps it is from the books he reads, or all the time he has to himself with no distractions, so that he is able to just think for hours on end. It more than likely is a combination. Oh, sometimes he'll allow his boyish side seep through, such as whenever a spider happens to appear on the stone wall, reminding him once more of my fear. Those moments are becoming further and further apart, however. I have probably seen him smile, *really* smile, maybe once or twice. Mostly his face is sad or expressionless. Whenever he manages to make me feel inferior despite the fact that I am older, he lets a smirk cross his face, sometimes paired with a raised eyebrow. I always end up embarrassed and angry in these moments, and my departure follows within seconds. *So what if I'm just letting him win?* I think to myself as I walk through the corridors to my bed.

One of his most noticeable requests has been for mirrors of every size and shape. I cannot help but wonder what a boy who hides behind a mask all the time would want with a mirror, let alone twenty. He has made it quite clear that it is not my place to question, however, only to obey. It has been a few weeks since he stopped asking for mirrors, and I am still questioning his reason when I see his boat approaching. I start to point out his tardiness, but then dismiss the idea. I already know what he is going to say. I start to hand him the sacks, but he does not reach for them. I look at him, puzzled, and his face registers a careful excitement. "Get in the boat. I want you to see something." I back away.

"No thank you, Erik...I'm quite content to remain right here."

"Are you sure?" He raises an eyebrow, and I think I catch a sparkle in his eye.

"Yes, I'm sure." *No, not really, now that you mention it.* He smirks before looking over my shoulder at the wall. *Uh oh.* I can already guess what he is looking at, but I look anyway. Yes, there is a huge spider, just above my shoulder, as if Erik had planned for it to be there right at this moment. I race forward.

"Ah. I see you've changed your mind."

"Oh, make it quick. There is a curfew, you know." I roll my eyes and follow him into the boat, and he pushes off. I sit stiffly in my seat in front of him. He rounds a curve around the stairs, landing the boat shortly after. He helps me out, and we walk silently down a set of passageways.

"Close your eyes," he orders.

"I most certainly will not!"

"Close them." He growls, and I do as he says. I feel him place his hands on my shoulder, guiding me forward several steps. "Now, open." As my eyes adjust, I see that I am immediately faced with several copies of myself. A room full of mirrors. Flashing another of his smirks, Erik steps away and out of sight.

"Now, Erik, that's not funny! Where are you?" I spin around, and it seems like the mirrors are spinning as well. Erik appears for a split second, but disappears as soon as I move towards him. He is laughing now, but it is impossible to follow his voice as it seems to echo off of every wall. "Erik, I am serious! Stop it this very instant!" I am trying not to cry. I will not give him the satisfaction. But I am getting dizzier by the second, and finally I fall to the floor.

"Would you like me to show you the way out?" He is next to me now. I want to reach out and punch his ankles. But I was raised better than that.

"Please do." He might be reaching down to help me up, but I won't let him. Only when I am standing on my own two feet to I reach out to touch his shoulder, and he leads me down the correct path and to a darkened corridor I've never seen before.

"I felt I should warn you about my newest trap." *Newest? There's more?* I do not voice my concern. Surprisingly, he continues. "Back in the carnival, before I was completely locked up...there was a house of mirrors. It was my favorite."

"You must have worked hard on that." My comment is met with a simple shrug, and the conversation ends just as quickly as it began. Silently, we make our way down the corridor, until he stops at what appears to be a dead end.

"Pull the lever. It leads to a set of stairs. I believe it will take you to the dorm rooms." I turn to thank him, but he is gone. It occurs to me just now that he mentioned the dorm rooms by name, and not the opera house in general. I have never thought to count the number of passageways there are throughout the opera house walls. I only knew of the one that leads down to the cellars, but apparently there is more than one. If there are others, surely they are in some state of disrepair, and should Erik plan on making use of all of them, he has quite a bit of work ahead of him. I can only hope that he remembers to remain hidden, and that his work will go unnoticed.

It has been a month since Erik showed me the mirror room. He has not said a word about it since then, except that there is now a trap door in the main lobby floor that leads straight down into it. How he managed that while still remaining hidden, I shall never know.

My mind has been on other things, anyway. The man who usually delivers our food has fallen ill, and his son has taken over for him. His name is Henri Giry, and we have met once or twice. We have not said more than polite greetings in passing, but I find him quite handsome, for a delivery boy.

I have my love for mornings to blame(or thank) for my knowledge of our deliveries. For as long as I can remember, I have always awakened an hour before the other dancers, when the stage hands are still sleeping off the previous night's indulgence, and when I have the opera house almost to myself. I spend these moments routinely, first by stretching and doing a simple dance, and then making my way toward the kitchen. It is not that I seek an extra handout, mind you. Us dancers are kept on a strict diet, and I have always found it very satisfying. Rather, it is the company of the cook staff I am looking for. The head cook is like a second mother to me, always friendly, and I can talk to her about anything. She is busy in the mornings, of course, between deliveries and breakfast preparations, but she makes time for me. The rest of the kitchen staff are friendly towards me as well, and if Paulette is really too busy, I can always count on them for pleasant conversation.

This morning, I finish my dance exercise slightly earlier than usual and quickly brush my fingers through my hair. It is Henri's day to be here, but I mustn't appear over-eager. To do so would invite unwelcome attention, as I have witnessed from other girls falling victim to one drunken stagehand or another. However, even though I hardly know Henri, I doubt he is like those men. Still, one cannot be too sure. I casually walk down the corridor, and sure enough, Henri has just brought a crate into the kitchen. "Good morning, Mademoiselle!" He smiles at me and tips his hat, and I feel myself blush.

"Good morning." *Stop staring, for goodness sake!* I look down at the counter in front of me, searching for something, *anything*, significant enough to have caused my sudden change of focus. Unfortunately, my eyes find nothing, and I inwardly scold Paulette for keeping the kitchen so clean! I hear his footsteps approaching me, but I do not look up. Instead, I beg my face to return to a normal color.

"For a beautiful dancer." He places a shiny red apple down in front of me.

"Oh, why thank you, Monsieur!" I finally look at his face, instantly taking notice of his deep blue eyes. *Oh, stop it, Antoinette, just stop it!*

"Please, call me Henri. And what might I call you?"

"A—Antoinette, Monsieu—uh, Henri..." There goes my face again. I am at least able to suppress a giggle.

"Pleased to meet you, Antoinette." He is extending his hand, and I take it. Instead of merely shaking it, he places my hand to his lips.

"Henri? Come now, there's a few more crates on your wagon." Paulette saves me from melting, and at her voice Henri drops my hand. As he disappears through the back door, Paulette looks at me with a raised eyebrow, then grins. Oh, dear, am I *that* transparent?

The giddiness I feel inside follows me down into the caverns tonight. Erik must sense it, for he is looking at me with a puzzled expression on his face. He does not question me, and I do not explain. However, I am sure he sees me bounce back up the stairs, as it was I, not he, who departed first.

Chapter Five: Erik Learns About Love

Two years. It is two years later, and it seems that the sudden change in Antoinette is not going to disappear anytime soon. Yes, even now, I can hear her long before I see her. She is humming her way down the stairs, not missing a note as she steers clear of the trap door. Her voice is not exceptional, but it is not bad at all either, considering she is only a dancer. As she comes into view, I see that she is dancing after all, to whatever tune she is humming. It is not one I recognize. "Do you write songs now, Antoinette?" She is surprised by my question as she hands me the usual sacks.

"Write songs? Me? Why, don't be silly, Erik!" Ah. She is attempting to make *me* seem foolish for once.

"Well, if it's not that, then what on earth were you humming just now?" I do not why my voice is coming out so harsh. Perhaps it is frustration of not knowing what's in her head.

"Oh, just something..." She waves her hand dismissively and continues her dance. I cannot stand it anymore.

"For goodness sake, girl, what has gotten into you?"

"Oh, Erik...I think...I think I'm in love..." She is biting her lip, and her cheeks are bright red.
Love? *Love?* The word is completely foreign to me. How dare she have this knowledge of something that I've never heard of!

"Whatever does that mean?" My question is met with laughter. *Laughter!* Of all the sounds I loathe, this one is certainly at the top of the list! It is a sound I had thought I was safe from hearing ever again. Apparently, I was wrong.

"Oh, Erik, you're such a...such a *boy!*" That does it. She may have helped me all these years, but I will not, *will not*, be talked down to in *my*home! I place my hands around her neck, and she finally sees the look in my eyes. Her laughter stops, and fear replaces the carefree expression. I drop my hands, but not my gaze. "F—forgive me, Erik...I wasn't thinking." She turns from me and begins pacing. I hear her sigh before she speaks again. "Love is...the most wonderful feeling in the world. There are different kinds of love, of course. There's the love a mother has for her child...there's the love between two friends...and then there's the 'in-love' sort of love. It's when a man and a woman admire and care for each other so much that they want to spend the rest of their lives together." She turns once again to face me, but she seems to be staring at something far in the distance. "Erik, one day you'll understand. I myself didn't fully understand the concept until I met Henri..." There she goes, biting her lip again. My thoughts, however, are elsewhere. *How can I come to understand? My own mother did not "love" me, what makes you think that anyone else will?* Suddenly, the cave seems too crowded. I throw the sacks into the boat, leaving Antoinette behind with no explanation. She won't understand anyway. No one will ever understand.

It has been a week, and I am staying right here. Antoinette can leave the sacks and go, because I will not see her. How can I possibly face her, knowing that she is so much more happier than I can ever hope to be? Oh, she might swallow her giggles and aimless tunes, she might hide her grins and far-off glances, but I'll know. I'll know that she pities me. *Pity.* I used to crave it. Now I know how patronizing it really is. I do not need pity. Not from her. Not from *anyone.*

Two weeks, and my food supply other than fish has run out. *Fine.* I reluctantly take my boat to the steps. Four sacks are waiting for me, but she is nowhere. *All the better.* There is a note on top of one of the sacks.

"Erik,

I cannot keep this up much longer without drawing attention to myself regarding the disappearances of food and materials. If you've found passageways throughout the opera house, it is high time you started using them and getting things for yourself. If not, I have a very small allowance as far as finances go, but I'm only supposed to use it for emergencies. If you think you're so clever, I suggest making a plan as soon as possible. I'll back you whatever you decide. Just let me know...you cannot hide from me forever.

Sincerely, Antoinette."

She really should have thought of this before. I believe she would have, too, if not for her 'love', Henri. Honestly, if loving someone gets in the way of rational thinking, I want no part of it!

When she returns the following week, I am waiting for her. I do not wait for her to speak. "To answer your question, yes, I have found several passageways, and yes, I have been working on repairing them. However, if you are very eager to discontinue our meetings, then by all means, go to your dear Henri and forget about me. I'll manage just fine."

"It's not that I want to, Erik. The fact is, when I brought you here, I had no idea that it would be for this long. I've only gone with the flow, taking things as they come. It's been years now, and we've both grown. You didn't honestly think that this could go on forever, did you?" I turn my face from her searching eyes. "Erik, just because you've settled quite nicely into a life down here doesn't mean that my life isn't going to change. I...I have dreams, I have needs..."

"And I don't? You don't think that I dream of life without...without THIS?" I tear the mask off my face, standing mere inches from her own face.

"I'm sorry Erik. Of course you do...it's just..." There are tears in her eyes. Why? What could she possibly have to cry about? I turn and walk away, placing the mask back on my face.

"Bringing me here was a mistake. You do not have to say it, I can see it in your eyes. I have become a burden to you."

"No, Erik, that's not what I am saying at all! If I hadn't brought you here, where else could you have gone? Where else would you have been safe?" She is touching my shoulder now. "Erik, I consider you a friend. Even though our meetings are only once a week, you are probably the closest friend I have. Yes, the opera house is full of girls, but there is always competition for the limelight. Every girl wants a part of it, and they will do anything, even sacrifice friendship, to get it."

"So what are the tears for? Why must the meetings end?"

"Forget the tears. You would not understand."

"*I* wouldn't understand *tears*?" I scoff.

"I said forget them!" Her harshness takes me aback, but only for a moment. She dries her tears before continuing. "I already told you that I will no longer be responsible for the disappearances in the opera house. I am glad you have found passageways. Perhaps now you can move on as well as I."

"If I am as close a friend as you say, then why must the meetings end just because I have the passageways? Tell me that!"

"It's just too dangerous! I am surprised that I have been able to go this long without anyone noticing me sneaking down here!"

"That's not true, Antoinette! If you were so worried about that, you would have stopped years ago!" She is really sobbing now, but I don't care anymore. If this so-called friendship is as fragile as she is implying, it is better for me to remove my emotions from it as soon as possible.

"Fine! You really want to know the reason?"

"Would I have asked if I did not?"

"I'm in love, Erik! Henri is a wonderful man and we love each other. Love like ours does not happen every day, and so when it does, it must become my main focus. I cannot afford to lose him."

"So you think that by coming here, you risk losing him."

"Exactly. I'm sorry, Erik. I did not mean to fall in love, but that fact is, I have fallen in love. That's not something we can ignore. So by all means, repair your passageways. I feel our meetings will end before the year is over."

I have been working in the passageways for a month now. The one behind the kitchen walls are the last of them, and I believe that tonight, they will be finished. I am filling in some gaps between the stones when I hear whispered voices. One belongs to Antoinette. The other voice is a man's, and I feel the hairs on the back of my neck bristle. I bend down and peer through the gap, confident that I am unnoticed. Antoinette is smiling, so this must be her precious Henri. Despite my disgust at his flawless face, this is an opportunity that cannot be missed. I remain in my position and listen. "Oh, Henri, that is horrible! I am so sorry!"

"Thank you, Antoinette, although we have seen it coming for a long time now. He was a very sick man, and he lived a full life. It was only a matter of time."

"Still, my dear, it must be painful for you."

"It is much easier with you here." The two embrace, and I feel as though I might be sick. "Of course, my beautiful dancer, this is a blessing in disguise. He has left the delivery business to me, which means I am much closer to having the means to support a wife, when the time comes."

"And how long might that take?"

"Not soon enough." They embrace again, and now I *know* I will be sick. They must not know I am here, however, and so I force myself to swallow the bitter taste in my mouth. Slowly, I make my way back down into the caverns.

As I approach our meeting place, my heart feels heavy. Something is going to happen tonight. I just know it. I land the boat and sit with my back to the stairs and my feet dangling in the water. As if on cue, I hear her footsteps descending into my darkness. I hear the sacks drop to the stone floor, but I do not reach for them. "Erik?" Her voice is quiet and cautious.

"You're leaving." It is not a question. I can hear it in her voice. She sighs in defeat.

"Yes, Erik. Henri has asked me to marry him."

"I suppose you said yes."

"Of course I did. I love him."

"I would think you would be happier about it then."

"I cannot be happy if you are not." I turn to face her, and my gaze immediately falls on her tear-filled eyes. "You are my best friend, Erik. I would hope you could at least be happy for me."

"Why should I? You're leaving! You're abandoning me!" Tears threaten to fill my own eyes, but I force them back, replacing them with sheer rage.

"Erik, for goodness sake, you are quite capable of living on your own. You have passageways to every corner of the opera house! You don't need me anymore!"

"You're right. I don't need you. I never have." My voice is an icy growl. It is a lie, of course, but I am not about to admit it. "Go! Go now and leave me!" With that, I get in the boat and sail into the shadows. I can easily return for the last couple of sacks, long after she is gone.

Chapter Six: Antoinette's New Future

I step into the dark corridor for the first time in five years. I am cold, whether from the emptiness inside me or the air around me, I cannot tell. What I do know is that I need time to think, and there is no better place than my old friend's darkness. I do not expect him to be there. Why should he, if he does not even know that I have returned? Even if he does know, he made it quite clear years ago that he does not care. I would have liked a better good bye to him, after all we've been through. But no, if there is one thing I can count on in Erik, it is his stubbornness.

I walk to the lake's edge, tears in my eyes that haven't completely stopped ever since I received the news. I am standing there, staring off into the distance, when a familiar voice sounds from behind me. "Beware of spiders." As I turn to look at him, the first thing I notice is how tall he has gotten. Even from several feet away, he towers above me, dressed in his usual black suit. He has made a few additions, particularly a black wig and cape and a white porcelain mask. "You're back."

"Yes...Henri was in an accident...he is dead..." I cannot keep the tears back, and they flow freely down my face. Erik does not reach out to console me, and I do not expect him to. He stands there, watching me and shifting his weight uncomfortably. He does not know what to do, I suppose, and so he is growing impatient with me. I force myself to still the tears, just enough to speak clearly. "The funeral is not until the spring...the ground is too frozen now."

"Will you return to the stage?"

"Of course not. I have a daughter now. No, I saw that they were in need of a ballet mistress. Perhaps my daughter will dance, when she is old enough."

"How old is she now?"

"Three years last Tuesday. Marguerite Annabelle Giry is her name."

"It's long for such a little girl."

"Yes...usually I call her Meg."

"You should go back to her."

"She is napping. How are you, Erik?" I meet his eyes now, and he glances down.

"I've managed."

"Erik, if you want me to apologize, I will not. You cannot fault me for falling in love."

"What's done is done." He shrugs and moves to stand beside me. We do not speak, only stare across the shadowy lake. "You need to understand that things have changed around here. What we had before...friendship, as you called it...can no longer happen."

"Erik, I..."

"Silence! From here on out, you will refer to me as the Opera Ghost, although some call me the Phantom of the Opera." My jaw drops at his words.

"People know about you?"

"It was not something I planned on, I can assure you of that. I was in one of my passageways when one of the dancers must have heard me. Acting like a ghost was the first thing that came to mind."

"Oh, Erik, must you frighten them? Those dancers have enough to worry about without a so-called ghost sneaking around!"

"Did I not tell you to call me Opera Ghost?" The familiar flash of anger appears in his eyes, and I involuntarily take a step back. "Besides. I do not go upstairs often, and when I do, it is for more important reasons than playing with the minds of the dancing girls."

"See that it's not. I am now responsible for those girls, and I-"

"You think I would put those girls in danger? What do you take me for, Antoinette?"

"A man who does not know his own strength." I meet his eyes evenly. "And if you have any passageways behind the walls of the dormitories, you had better tell me now."

"There are some, yes..." He seems shocked at my bravery.

"I forbid you from using them. You must promise to allow the girls to have their privacy."

"You have my word." Just as suddenly as it appeared, the shock melts away. "Now you will hear my demands. You will not come down here again unless I send for you. I have been in communication with the manager through notes I place in various locations, and I will begin sending you notes as well. Furthermore, you must know that I have demanded Box Five to be left empty for my use."

"Box Five! Do you know how expensive that is?"

"I am able to afford it." He is hiding something. I can see it in his shifting eyes.

"How?" We are both surprised by the growl in my voice. He lets out a sigh.

"The manager pays me a small salary every month. It is for materials and emergencies that might arise."

"And what do you do to earn this salary?"

"It is simple. I allow the show to go on." His mouth twists into a mischievous smirk.

"Exactly how small a salary is it?" I swallow the scream that threatens to escape my lips. *Blackmail!* But of course he does not know any better, and he certainly won't listen to me if I try to explain it.

"Only twenty thousand francs."

"Why Erik, that's..."

"I swear to you Antoinette, if you dare utter that name again..." His threatening tone shatters my train of thought. "You must refrain from using my real name, else you give my secret away. You have been careful before, but now that my presence is known, it would only be a matter of time before your tongue slips. If it's easier, you may call me 'O.G.'."

"Very well."

"Now then, there are several smaller passageways throughout the opera house that I will allow you to use, to keep an eye on the girls. I will show them to you in time. For now, go to your daughter." With a dismissive wave of his hand, he is gone.

"Mme. Giry,

Enclosed are several bills that you will deposit in the bank of your choosing. From here on, you will collect my salary and deposit exactly ninety percent in your name. You may take five percent for your own use, and place the remaining funds behind the curtains of Box Five.

Sincerely,

O.G."

For one who did not plan to be heard, he has certainly embraced the role of a ghost, I think to myself as I study the red skull seal. I found the envelope in the prop room, and I cannot help but wonder how he knew I would be going in there today. Even with the note removed, the envelope is extremely thick. I reach in and pull out a massive stack of bills, oh so much more than I have ever seen in my life. *Deposit it? In my name? Would that not raise suspicion?* No, I cannot do it. I cannot risk anyone asking questions. *Think, Antoinette, think!* My thoughts turn to my daughter, who is at this very moment following the dancers around. The older girls know by now to help me keep an eye on her, but her three-year-old curiosity is starting to make me nervous.

All of a sudden, inspiration strikes, and I call out to one of the older chorus girls. "Jeanette! Would you mind watching Meg for a few minutes? I have an errand to run."

"Of course, Madame Giry." Jeanette's eager grin remind me of how well she gets along with my daughter. My mind at ease, I hurry off to the bank to open an account in Meg's name.

It is before dawn when I enter the stables. Erik is there, just as planned, blending in with the shadows. When I first approached him with my request, I was met with all-out refusal. Only with non-stop persistence on my part is he here now. I silently motion him towards one of the empty carriages, and once he is inside I go to fetch the driver.

Only when we are on our way does he speak. "Why of all people do you need *me* here?" I am glad he is keeping his voice low; Meg has not yet awakened and is using my lap for a pillow.

"Because whether or not you like it, you are my oldest and dearest friend. I wouldn't think of coming without you." It is something I've been repeating all along, and he still will not accept it. "Besides, as I said, it will be a small, private funeral. Other than us, only Henri's mother and sister will be there." He does not respond, and I do not know if I prefer his silence or his arguments. He is staring out the carriage window, and I can only wonder what is going through his mind. After all, it has been ten years since he has been outside the opera house.

We arrive at the graveyard with plenty of time to spare. The cemetery is covered in a thick fog, and I am sure my friend is thankful for the added 'mask' to hide in. Even now, as we approach the grave site, he is holding back. I feel that I should say something, anything, to reassure him that his presence is more than welcome, but I see the undertaker's carriage arriving. Henri's family is not far behind. Meg chooses this moment to wake up, and she immediately starts crying for her breakfast. I suddenly feel overwhelmed and light-headed. *This was not supposed to happen. None of this. Henri was young...it's too soon...* Suddenly, a black leather-gloved hand reaches out toward Meg, and in it is a small crust of bread. I search Erik's face for an explanation. "I brought it along just to nibble on. It appears as though she needs it more than I do."

"Thank you." The words are few, but I hope that he sees in my face exactly how grateful I am. He is no longer looking at me, however, and I follow his gaze until I see my late husband's family approaching us.

"Who is this?" Henri's mother questions. Out of the corner of my eye, I see Erik shift his weight uncomfortably. For the first time, I have second thoughts about inviting him here.

"This is an old friend of mine, from my childhood."

"Erik." He surprises me by extending his hand, as if he was raised to be a gentleman. I am more surprised, however, that he has given his real name. But then, introducing one's self as 'Opera Ghost' at a funeral is hardly appropriate. My thoughts shift again as Henri's coffin is brought to the grave site. Although I am already holding Meg's hand tightly, I give it an extra squeeze as I absentmindedly walk over to it.

Throughout the small service, all my attention is on the tears I am shedding and the love of my life gone too soon. At some point, Erik slips away to hide in the carriage. I only notice his absence when Meg moves to follow him. I will not let her, however. This is her father we are burying, after all, not to mention I am unsure as to the state of mind Erik is in. He is in a strange place full of strangers, and only here because I would not let him refuse. The time soon comes for me to place my single red rose on the wooden box. I do so slowly and reluctantly, adding a small caress to the lid. "Good bye, my love," I whisper.

My feet stay planted until the fresh mound of dirt is complete. I barely notice my in-laws leaving, and I mumble a polite good bye. I am sure that they understand...even so, I make a silent vow to visit them every now and again. I let go of Meg's tiny hand; she knows not to go running off. Instead, she decides to fall asleep in the nearby grass. If I was not in tears right now, I would scold her for getting stains on her nice black dress. Instead, I stare at my husband's grave, wishing I could feel just once more his strong arms around me as he whispers in my ear, "I love you, my beautiful dancer." A fresh wave of tears washes over me now, and I place my face in my hands. I hear his footprints before I feel his hand gingerly touch my shoulder.

"He was not supposed to die, Erik! He was so young..." His name slips out before I can stop it, but for once, he does not scold me.

"You must be strong. For Meg's sake."

"I know...It's just so hard...I loved him so much!"

"At least...you have Meg..."

"Yes, I have Meg." I sigh. "And I know her beauty will match his handsomeness." His hand stiffens, but again, he does not scold me. Even so, he did not deserve that. "I'm sorry."

"Don't ever be sorry for stating the truth, Antoinette. Now come...we must return so Meg can finish her nap in a proper bed." I wipe the tears from my eyes while he picks the sleeping child up. Silently, we walk back to the carriage. Once I am seated, he hands my daughter over to me before taking his own seat. As we are leaving, I keep my gaze on the mound of dirt until it is out of sight.

Chapter Seven: Transition and a Promise

Author's Note: As this is the uneven last chapter, I've switched perspective and changed it to third-person.

Over the next few weeks, Antoinette mainly kept to herself. One of the more advanced dancers took over the majority of her duties without her needing to ask, and she was equally grateful that Erik did not send for her. Even though he had never experienced a loss such as this, he seemed to understand that she had not yet had a proper grieving period, between selling their house, moving back to the opera house, and stepping into the roll of ballet mistress. Even sweet, little Meg seemed much calmer around her mother during these long weeks. Jeanette often arrived at Madame Giry's quarters soon after breakfast to take Meg on strolls around the theater. Paulette soon followed with a breakfast tray, from which Antoinette only took a few bites before curling up on her bed.

She sometimes thought of going to the kitchen for lunch, but the idea was always quickly dismissed. After all, it was there that she and Henri met, and so it would be far too painful to face those memories just yet.

And so, when her tears dried and the pain had somewhat subsided, she danced. She danced to the music of her pain and her uncertainty of the future. She danced to the music of the silence, relishing the moments she had all to herself. And then the memories came rushing back to her, reminding her of her loss and her new responsibilities, and she would collapse on the bed for yet another crying spell.

On one particular afternoon, her crying spell was interrupted by Jeanette bursting into the room, her own tears flooding down her cheeks. "Oh, Madame Giry...I only took my eyes off her one second! One second!" The panic in her voice was contagious, and Antoinette's tears quickly dried.

"Jeanette, you must control yourself! What exactly happened?"

"We were down the corridor outside the dressing rooms. Everything was fine. She was babbling on about one of the dance routines, at least that's what I could make of it. Just then some of the stagehands appeared with a heavy set piece...I quickly moved out of the way...when they were gone, so was she!"

"Did you check the dressing rooms or question the stagehands?" Antoinette knew she had to remain calm, as an example to the younger woman, despite the screams that threatened to emerge from her very soul.

"The stagehands saw nothing...and I did check the dressing rooms, and they were all empty!"

"Please, Jeanette, do calm down. Go to the kitchen and ask for a cup of tea. Once you feel better, go see if Monsieur Reyer will work with you on your solo."

"Yes, Madame. And I truly am sorry..." Jeanette exited the room with her head hung, and Antoinette said a silent prayer before beginning her own search.

The sound of a wailing child broke Erik's concentration. For a moment, he thought it was a ghost from his past, echoing the pain he had felt so many times before. But no, these belonged to a girl, one much younger than he had been at that time. With a frustrated sigh, he reluctantly abandoned the trap he had been working on and followed the voice up the spiral staircase. Once he reached the source, he stopped dead in his tracks. It was none other than little Meg Giry, sitting on the slightly damp floor and clutching her knee. *Where in the world is her mother?* Anger flared up inside him. He himself had been neglected by his mother, and he did not wish that on his worst enemy, let alone this little innocent girl. *Alright, you've established your feelings, now what are you going to do about it?* He hated when his thoughts did that. But as always, they had a point, and he studied the situation before him. Finally, shaking inside, he got down to her level and attempted to appear as non-frightening as possible. She brought her tiny head up to face him, and the first thing he noticed was how big and blue her eyes were. "I...fall...down..." she managed through breathless sobs. He was speechless. What did she want him to do? That is, what did she want him to do that would not put her in danger? Finally, he began humming a tune he had been working on. He did not have any words to it yet, but he found the tune quite soothing. Apparently, Meg felt the same, and her tears soon slowed down. "I want..Mama..."

"Let's go find her then." He gently picked her up and lifted himself onto his feet. He immediately knew where they were, and began making his way back to the mirror-door that led to one of the dressing rooms. For a moment, he hesitated before stepping through. It was the middle of the afternoon, in broad daylight. Anyone could be walking by and see him.

"My knee...hurts..." Meg's words made up his mind for him, and he slid open the door. Almost instantly, Antoinette was in front of him, grabbing her daughter out of his arms.

"There, there, Marguerite...I'm here..." Antoinette spoke softly as her daughter clung tightly to her neck.

"Mama...I fall down...knee hurt..."

"Let's go into the kitchen. I'm sure Paulette will have something for you." Antoinette brushed her hand across Meg's tear-stained face. "O.G., wait in that corridor. I must speak with you."

"And I have words of my own, Madame Giry." Erik allowed the coolness in his voice to sink in before he disappeared in a swish of his cape.

As soon as Paulette saw the sobbing child, she gathered Meg up into her arms. "Aww...did someone skin their knee? Well, we'll just have to fix that up, won't we?"

"Thank you, Paulette. Would you keep a close eye on her for me? Don't let her leave this room? There's some urgent business I need to take care of."

"No need to explain. I'll take good care of her."

"I know you will. I won't be long." Antoinette managed a half-smile before swiftly making her way back to the dressing room. *Erik, you had better have a very good explanation for this!*

For the longest time after they were face to face again, neither one spoke. They allowed their eyes to do the talking for them, and both looks were that of accusation. Finally, it was Antoinette who broke the silence. "O.G., I want answers, and I want them *now!* What was Meg doing back here?"

"Your guess is as good as mine. But I can assure you, had you been doing your duty as her mother, this would never have happened!"

"How *dare* you tell *me* how to raise *my own* daughter!" Antoinette brought her hand up and slapped his face. As soon as the contact was made, she deeply regretted it, but it was too late. Erik shook the initial shock off, then took her by the shoulders and began shaking her. "Erik, stop it! Please!" Erik took one look at her eyes, and his grip loosened. He turned his back to her, choosing to ignore the sound of her catching her breath.

"You should know by now that I will not be struck ever again without there being severe consequences." Antoinette sighed. This was as close to an apology as she was going to get.

"And I will have *you* know that I am Meg's mother, and I will do anything to protect her."

"I was doing nothing! I would never, ever harm her!"

"I wish I could believe you, Erik, but your most recent outburst gives me cause to doubt. Until you learn to control that temper of yours, I want you to promise to stay away from my daughter."

"I thought I told you to call me O.G."

"*Erik*, promise me." They were exchanging glares again, but this time, Erik was the one who spoke first.

"I'll give my word on one condition, and you *will* hear me out. It is obvious that we both care for

Meg's safety very deeply. And so you will promise me that you will not let Meg out of your sight. I know your dear husband died and you miss him, but don't allow that to overshadow the fact that you have a daughter who depends on you to be there for her." As he spoke, Antoinette could only guess at where these words were coming from. But of course. He had been neglected. It all made sense.

"I promise." She spoke softly, but she meant every word.

"Then I promise." They shook hands, and before anymore words could be spoken, he disappeared in a dramatic swish of his cape.

As the year passed, Antoinette's crying spells diminished, and she was soon able to resume her normal duties as Meg's mother and as the ballet mistress. Erik wasted no time continuing to send messages to and through her. At first, Antoinette found it cruel, but when she realized it was helping her to think outside her grief, she found she could not be angry with him. Oh, she still missed Henri, to be sure, and sometimes she was so overwhelmed by the memories that she would cry herself to sleep, but she did not let that consume her. Instead, she vowed to raise Meg to be a daughter Henri would have been proud of. *After all,* she thought, *if he is looking down and watching me, he would not want to see me wasting away to nothing but a pool of tears.*

Erik, in turn, watched the world pass by from behind stone walls and the Box Five curtains. Although he never said it aloud, he felt a small amount of pride toward Antoinette as she emerged from her sorrow and stuck to her daughter like glue. Not only did he hate to see Meg left alone, he hated to see Antoinette so sad. Of course, he would never admit it, and if that thought rose up in his mind, he shoved it right back down. It wasn't long before he could put his mind at ease about Meg's welfare, and she soon blended in with the rest of the little girls, especially once she was old enough to join the ballet.

Whenever inspiration refused to strike as far as his music was concerned, he went on strolls through the passageways or played tiny harmless pranks on whomever looked as though they deserved one. These pranks were the one thing he kept Antoinette in the dark about. If anyone other than himself knew of them, the element of surprise would be completely ruined.

Inspiration often came from watching rehearsals and performances from Box Five. When he first demanded it to be reserved for himself, a small trickle of cast and crew members attempted to sneak a peek at the Opera Ghost. Erik always saw them coming, however, and from his hiding spot behind the curtains, he still made his presence known by making what he hoped were ghost-like sounds. His only regret was not being able to laugh aloud at their retreating figures.

Erik enjoyed one evening in particular. It was during Antoinette's third year as the ballet mistress, and the manager was putting on a small private New-Year's Eve concert for his most faithful(and most wealthy) opera-goers, and the special guest musician was a violinist from Sweden. Gustave Daae was apparently very well-known in the outside world, and Erik was very eager to hear another master of the instrument. He heard it mentioned that Antoinette was asked to watch the violinist's daughter, Christine, during the rehearsals and final performance, but he was not the least bit interested in anything about their guest except how well he played, and if his talents matched his reputation. After all, to him, Christine Daae was just another little girl running around the opera house.

Gustave's performance lived up to Erik's expectation. He would not allow himself to be too pleased by his talent, however. After all, his own music was extremely precious to him, and he would not let himself be threatened by any other musician, let alone a foreigner.

The pleasantness surrounding Monsieur Daae's visit was short-lived, however. In the week that followed the concert, word soon arrived that the Swedish violinist had fallen ill. He was staying with the manager a few blocks from the opera house, and it was solemnly announced that the doctor had not given him very much time to live. Antoinette was asked to spend some time living there; Gustave had requested that his daughter go to live in the opera house once he was gone, and it was agreed that Antoinette was the right choice to help Christine with the transition. Antoinette immediately felt pity toward the little girl, who was the same age as her own daughter. And so, she gingerly but urgently sent a message down to Erik, hoping that he would understand her absence.

"I managed five years without you here, Antoinette. I believe I can take care of myself." Erik scoffed in reply. They were in the corridor behind the mirror.

"Yes, well, I just wanted to give you warning that Meg and I won't be around. I cannot tell you when we will be back."

"You don't think I know everything that goes on within this opera house? I was already well-aware of your plans."

"Very well. We will be leaving in the morning. And, O.G.," Antoinette allowed a smile to appear on her face. "Don't do anything rash while I'm gone. I cannot very well bring Christine to a burnt-down opera house or anything like that." She made sure he caught the lightheartedness of her tone.

"Why on earth would I burn my own house down, Antoinette? Honestly." Erik matched her smile—he even allowed a chuckle to escape his throat. "You just watch out for spiders." A flash of mischievousness passed over his face, and with that, the two went their separate ways.

Made in the USA
Monee, IL
16 November 2025